Hell Squad: Hemi

Anna Hackett

Hemi

Published by Anna Hackett
Copyright 2017 by Anna Hackett
Cover by Melody Simmons of eBookindiecovers
Edits by Tanya Saari

ISBN (eBook): 978-1-925539-22-6
ISBN (paperback): 978-1-925539-24-0

What readers are saying about Anna's Science Fiction Romance

At Star's End – One of Library Journal's Best E-Original Romances for 2014

Return to Dark Earth – One of Library Journal's Best E-Original Books for 2015 and two-time SFR Galaxy Awards winner

The Phoenix Adventures – SFR Galaxy Award Winner for Most Fun New Series and "Why Isn't This a Movie?" Series

Beneath a Trojan Moon – SFR Galaxy Award Winner and RWAus Ella Award Winner

Hell Squad – Amazon Bestselling Science Fiction Romance Series and SFR Galaxy Award for best Post-Apocalypse for Readers who don't like Post-Apocalypse

The Anomaly Series – #1 Amazon Action Adventure Romance Bestseller

.

Chapter One

"I cannot *believe* that moron," Camryn McNab muttered.

From behind her on the Hawk quadcopter, she heard snickers from her squad mates. She whipped around to glare at them. God, even their leader—rough, rugged Roth Masters—was grinning.

"It is not funny," she insisted.

"I think it looks pretty," Sienna said. The small, curvy brunette looked like she should be in a kitchen baking, not decked out in carbon fiber armor, about to head into a battle with invading dinosaur-like aliens.

Cam pointed to the combat helmet on her head. "He put an *H* on my helmet...in *rhinestones*." Even though she couldn't see the offending letter, anger was a wild churn in her belly. The man could light the fuse on her temper faster than anyone she'd ever known. "And he glued them on with some high-tech adhesive." When they'd been prepping for their mission, and she'd discovered the tampering, she'd tried to pry the rhinestones off, but they weren't budging.

At the back of the Hawk, Taylor Cates started

laughing. Her dark hair was pulled back in a ponytail and as she doubled over, it fell over her shoulder. "Can you picture big, bad Hemi with sparkly rhinestones?" She held her middle as she laughed.

Beside Taylor, their second-in-command, Mackenna 'Mac' Carides, was biting her lip to fight back a laugh. Hell, even quiet, stubborn Theron was smiling. He'd been doing that a lot these last few days, since he and Sienna had turned from friends to lovers.

"Go ahead, laugh it up," Cam said darkly.

Hemi Rahia, bane of her existence, wouldn't know what hit him when she got back to base.

He was a soldier on Squad Three—a group of men also known as the berserkers, for their wild fighting style. He was also a big, muscled, tattooed, aggravating moron.

"Coming up on the targets," a male voice called back from the cockpit. Their top Hawk pilot, Finn Erickson, was at the controls today. Beneath her, Cam felt the quadcopter move into a turn.

Cam put any thought of pranks, revenge, and Hemi out of her head. It was time to focus on their mission.

Over a year and a half ago, aliens had invaded Earth. Almost overnight, she'd gone from a member of the United Coalition Airforce's Combat Support Squadron, protecting airfields, aircraft and personnel, to a member of Squad Nine.

Home was now a former underground coal mine, called the Enclave. All the fighting squads were made up of survivors from former military and police groups, or—in the case of the berserkers—people from questionable backgrounds who knew how to fight. Her squad consisted of a bunch of kickass ladies, their fearless leader Roth, and big, quiet Theron. They were tight, and she was proud as hell that they made an awesome team.

Now, they fought to protect the inhabitants of the Enclave, as well as to defeat the Gizzida. Her jaw tightened, and she pressed a hand against the wall of the Hawk. Cam liked fighting back. She looked out the side window at the setting sun. It was New Year's Eve, and she had no idea what the new year would bring. None of them did.

Would they finally be able to beat the Gizzida, and all the strange and terrifying creatures they used as weapons? Would humanity survive to rebuild their world?

She shook her head. Her thoughts were turning far too melancholy and deep.

"Let's get this mission done." They were off to destroy a large pack of hellions—alien hunting dogs, with poison-filled bellies. She straightened and looked at her friends. "I want to get back for the big party tonight."

Everyone at the Enclave was excited for the party. She knew how important it was for everyone to blow off a little steam, and celebrate all the little good things that they still managed to find in the middle of this alien apocalypse. Cam wanted to drink, dance, and find some hottie to kiss at midnight.

She recalled a certain moron had taunted her on their last mission to rescue Theron and Sienna from an alien encampment. In alpha-male style, he'd already claimed her New Year's kiss.

In your dreams, Rahia.

"I want to get back to the party, too," a deep voice said, interrupting her thoughts.

Cam narrowed her eyes suspiciously on Theron. The man hated parties. "You just want to bang Sienna's brains out."

Theron tilted his head, his face thoughtful. "Yep."

Since her friends had hooked up, they'd been inseparable. They were so damn perfect together. The big man and the sweet soldier. Cam saw pink fill Sienna's cheeks as she stared at her man.

It was sweet, but it wasn't for Cam. *No, no, no.* She was *not* built for long-term. Fun, easy, and sexy...that was what she liked, and frankly, all she could manage. She came from two people incapable of love.

No. That wasn't true. Her parents were only capable of toxic, soul-destroying love.

She felt the Hawk start to descend. Out the window, she could see a strange, red-orange glow ahead.

Roth shouldered in beside her. "What the hell is that?"

They were south of the Enclave, but the landscape still consisted of rolling, green hills. Between two hills was a large, pockmarked patch of ground. It looked like it had been bombarded by meteors. Each of the holes glowed orange from underground.

It reminded Cam of a trip she'd taken to Hawaii once, to see the lava field near the volcano on the Big Island.

But she knew this strangeness had nothing to do with volcanoes and everything to do with the aliens.

"Whatever it is, it's not our priority," Roth said. "I'll pass the intel on. For now, the drone team reported a large group of hellions in the area, and they're getting too close to the Enclave. We need to clean them out."

Mac swung her carbine off her shoulder. "Let's do this."

Moments later, the Hawk was hovering above the ground and Roth slid the side door open with one powerful shove. "Time to go hunting."

Cam leaped out, her boots hitting the grass. The sunset had turned the western horizon brilliant shades of orange and pink. She raised her carbine, the feel of it familiar under her gloved hands. She moved into formation with her squad, falling in behind Mac.

"Anyone see the hellions?" Mac murmured.

Cam saw green grass, clumps of trees in the distance near a farmhouse, and that eerie orange glow in the distance, but no mangy beasts.

"Squad Nine." The cool, feminine voice came through their earpieces. Arden was their comms officer, who sat back at base, feeding them intel. "You have a pack of ten hellions inbound."

"Ten?" Sienna shuddered.

"Be ready," Roth said, tone hard.

"There!" Mac yelled.

Off to the left, Cam heard the yips and snarls. A pack of scaled, spiked, alien dogs was bounding toward them. Each animal had a powerful body, spikes along its back, slavering jaws filled with sharp teeth, and glowing-red bellies filled with poison.

Squad Nine opened fire, green laser blasts whizzing through the twilight. Cam aimed, taking down the first alien hunting dog. Its belly burst open, spraying out corrosive red fluid. Other hellions fell, their angry snarls and howls of pain filling the air.

"Grenades out." Theron's deep voice.

Cam watched as the grenades sailed through the air. They were made with cedar oil, which for whatever reason, the hellions and the closely-related canids, found strongly repulsive.

As the grenades exploded, sending up a fine mist, she watched the hellions scatter in a chaotic frenzy, spinning and snapping at each other. Several turned and ran into the growing darkness.

"Take them down," Roth ordered.

"On it." Taylor was down on one knee, holding a long-range laser rifle. Cam watched as, one by one, the fleeing dogs fell. Taylor was good. She might even give Hell Squad's charming sniper, Shaw Baird, a run for his money.

"More hellions coming in from behind you," Arden said.

As soon as Arden spoke, a low growl reached Cam's ears. She spun and spotted the incoming hellions.

"On our six," Cam called out.

She fired on the animals, but these particular ones had wised up. They dodged the laser fire, bounding closer.

Roth lunged past her, a large combat knife in his hand. As one giant hellion leaped at him, he jumped into the air to meet it.

Roth was a badass. Cam swung her carbine onto her shoulder, and pulled her dual laser pistols from the holsters on her thighs.

As the other hellion came at her, she held her weapons up, walking calmly toward the creature as she fired.

Its belly exploded and she leaped back to avoid the sizzling poison. The red fluid splattered the ground, rapidly eating through the grass and dirt.

Cam turned and watched the final hellion fall under Sienna's carbine fire. Cam looked at Roth and saw him stand, then lean down to wipe the blood off his combat knife.

Cam sucked in a deep breath, adrenaline pumping thickly through her veins. Taylor smiled at her and Cam smiled back. All in a day's work for Squad Nine.

"All hellions on scans have been neutralized," Arden said. "Get back to base, Squad Nine."

"Arden, there is an area southwest of us," Roth said. "Pockmarked ground that's glowing orange. It has 'Gizzida' written all over it."

"Passing that intel on to the drone team. We'll have them investigate." The cool, elegant woman rarely sounded flustered. "For now, it's getting dark, and there have been reports of alien swarms just south of your location. Time to get back to base."

Cam kicked the carcass of a hellion out of her way. She did not want to run into a swarm of bat-like aliens that could pick flesh off bones in seconds. At least the suckers only came out at night. "Plus, we have a party to get to."

"There's the Hawk." Roth waved them toward the incoming quadcopter.

The Hawk had dropped its illusion, its gray hull visible. As it descended, it kicked up dust around them.

Cam leaped aboard, followed by her squad mates. As the Hawk rose, she turned back to stare at the strange orange glow in the distance. For a second, she thought she saw shadows moving over the glow. Then Roth slammed the door closed.

Shaking off a sense of foreboding, she turned to her friends. "Party time, people."

Sienna dropped into a seat, grinning. "I've got a super-sexy dress to wear tonight."

Cam watched Theron's gaze sharpen on his woman. Smiling, Cam dropped into her own seat, stretching her long legs out in front of her. She had a sexy little dress of her own to wear tonight. Not that she was dressing up for anybody. Just herself.

However, if an annoying, helmet-interfering jerk happened to see her, she was going to make sure he got a good, long look at what he couldn't touch.

She closed her eyes. A party was just what she needed. She'd dance, get a little buzz from some homebrewed beer, and she'd find some fun in the middle of this shitty alien apocalypse.

***

Hemi Rahia strode up to the large double doors. They swooshed open and he stepped into the Enclave's Command Center.

His squad mates and his brothers were already down at the New Year's Eve party, but Hemi had something he needed to do first before he joined them.

Through a glass wall, he saw the drone team operators hunched over the controls of the drones out in the field. But he pulled his gaze back. He wasn't interested in the drones today. He spied some of the comms officers sitting in front of their comp screens, and zeroed in on one dark head.

"Hey, Arden."

At the deep rumble of his voice, the brunette swiveled, her eyes widening. "Hemi."

She was pretty, in a neat, elegant way. Not Hemi's style, he preferred attitude and fire. But the one thing that caught him was what he saw in her eyes—a heartbreaking sadness.

He cleared his throat. "I'm after an update on Squad Nine's mission."

"It went fine. They're on their way home, and eager to get to the party."

Something tight in Hemi's gut eased a little. "Good."

A small smile tilted Arden's lips. "I heard about the rhinestones."

Hemi shoved his hands in the pockets of his cargo pants. "How mad was she?"

Arden pressed her tongue to her teeth. "Mad."

Hemi grinned. *Good.* He and Camryn had been circling each other for months. Most days, it felt like a fucking lifetime. The woman had personal armor stronger than carbon fiber. And she could run. Hell, she had the legs for it, that was for sure.

But tonight, it stopped. Tonight was the beginning of a new year. It was time for him and Cam to begin new things.

"Thanks, Arden," he said. "See you at the party."

Her smile dissolved. "Maybe. Happy New Year, Hemi."

He headed out of the Command Center and down the corridor in the direction of the dining room, where the party was being held.

Hemi knew winning the war against the aliens was a long shot, but he also knew that he, his brothers, the other soldiers—they'd never stop fighting. They'd fight to keep kids safe, to protect the survivors who'd made it this far, to give humanity a chance.

But that didn't mean life didn't go on.

He thought of his mother. His Ma had lost her husband and been left to raise three rambunctious boys alone. She hadn't complained, she'd just gotten on with it. Surrounded by family back home in New Zealand, she'd made a home for him and his brothers. And eventually, she'd met a good man, and Hemi had scored an amazing stepdad who'd instilled in him a strong sense of right and wrong.

And his Pa had also given him a great example of how you treated the woman who was your everything.

Hemi liked women, and liked being buried deep inside their warmth and softness. God, they smelled sweet. But his Pa had told him that with the right one, the one who was worth the trouble, everything was so much better.

And Hemi knew Camryn McNab was his.

Every gorgeous, courageous, attitude-filled inch of her.

Now he had to convince her of that...if only he could get her to stop running.

He heard the music and laughter coming from the dining room. He pulled up short. The room had been transformed. Blue-and-silver fairy lights flickered all around the darkened room. A disco strobe light cast bright sparkles across the packed dance floor. A few older couples were swaying beside a group of teens bumping and grinding to the music.

All of the dining hall's tables and chairs had been moved to one side of the room, and a large number of people were sitting, eating and drinking. Nearby several long tables were filled with food. He saw a huge black man with one arm missing near the tables, barking orders at some of the kitchen staff. Chef had run the kitchens at their old base in the Blue Mountains. He'd been injured on their race to the Enclave, but he was clearly getting back on his feet.

Hemi spotted his squad, grabbed a homebrewed beer from the buckets near the door, and headed their way.

They were a scary bunch of badasses. Big, tough, inked...and he'd never fought with a better team.

His brother, Tane, was sprawled in a chair, cradling a beer between his knees. He had his dreadlocks pulled back at the base of his neck, and his gaze was angled toward the dance floor. It looked like he was brooding.

Brooding was standard MO for Hemi's little bro. Tane had seen too much in the jungles of South America, working as a mercenary. Hemi had eventually gone to work with him, specializing in kidnap-victim recovery. They'd lost a few, and rescued a few who'd never be the same...hell, some of the stuff they'd seen was enough to turn Hemi's iron gut.

Still, nothing was as bad as the horrors the Gizzida cooked up in their labs.

Hemi turned his head to follow Tane's gaze. It didn't take him long to find the pretty little silver-haired woman. Their resident alien was dancing with the teens, her skin and hair glowing under the bright lights.

Selena had pale, silver-white hair, and even paler skin. Tonight, someone had decked her out in a glittery blue dress, and she was smiling. He grinned. The woman had no rhythm at all, but it looked like she was having fun. She was another person snatched by the raptors and abused, but since the squads had rescued her, she was slowly blooming. He couldn't imagine how it felt to be so far from your planet and everything you knew, with no way home.

Hemi looked back at his brother. Yes, Selena was blooming and his jaded, hard-ass brother seemed to be very aware of that. *Interesting.*

The rest of his squad mates were gathered nearby. Ash Connors was leaning against the wall, his colored ink displayed by the rolled-up sleeves of his dark shirt. The women fucking loved the man's pretty face, but for some reason, he was solo tonight. Come to think of it, Ash had been showing up solo for a while now.

Ash's best friend, Levi King, was sitting near his friend, a pretty, giggling schoolteacher in his lap. Levi's hair was pulled up in the man bun they all gave him hell for, and he was grinning indulgently at the woman.

The other two berserkers, Griff and Dom, were talking quietly. A couple of women were eying the two, trying to get up the courage to approach them. Hemi snorted. Yeah, good luck with that. The former cop and ex-con, and the former mafia enforcer were dangerous and moody as hell. He knew they fucked women when it suited them, but for the most part, they enjoyed doing the chasing.

His friends all fought hard, partied hard, and did whatever the fuck they wanted.

He scanned the room, trying to see if anyone from Squad Nine had arrived.

"Hey, Hemi."

A beautiful woman who barely reached his shoulder moved in close to him. Her dangerous curves were packed into a red dress and a cloud of dark hair curled around her face. He stifled a sigh. He'd fooled around with Sal a few times at Blue Mountain Base and she'd made it clear she wanted to take it further. The woman was nothing, if not persistent.

"Hey, Sal."

"Got any plans tonight?" She stroked her hand down his arm. "I'd like to rock your world to welcome in the new year."

"Generous, but I've got plans." He scanned the room again. Big plans.

Sal pouted, but nodded. Casual sex wasn't frowned on since the invasion. In a world gone to hell, where so many people had lost their loved ones, being close to someone was sometimes the only thing that helped get people through the long, dark nights.

And living confined in such a small space, people were forced into close proximity.

"Have a good one," he told her.

She looked back over her shoulder. "You're missing out." She blew him a kiss.

He sat down beside Tane and his brother raised a brow. "You have plans?"

"Yep." Hemi sipped his beer.

From behind him, Levi snorted. "About time.

Your balls must be blue by now, Rahia."

Hemi shot the man a finger. "You seem very worried about my balls, King."

Levi smiled. "We all know which sexy Amazon you're panting after. Can't say I blame you."

Hemi lunged out of his chair, but Tane grabbed his arm and yanked him back down.

Levi didn't even flinch. The man's grin just widened, and he sipped his drink.

Hemi knew his friend was just yanking his chain. He sat back, waiting and watching. He tried to calculate how long it would take Squad Nine to get back, and then shower and change. All around him, people were dancing and laughing and drinking. He spied a couple kissing wildly in a shadowed corner.

Finally, he saw Roth enter, with his arm around his partner, Avery. They headed over to where Hell Squad was hanging out.

Anticipation licked at Hemi's gut. She'd be here soon.

Next up, he saw Mac and Taylor appear. Both the women were looking gorgeous in slick little dresses of bronze and green, respectively. Mac made a beeline towards Niko, the Enclave's civilian leader. The man yanked his woman in for a hard kiss. Taylor was only a few steps behind, heading toward her man, Devlin.

Theron and Sienna appeared. The couple had only just tumbled head-over-ass in love, and they'd done it in the middle of a dangerous mission. Hemi and his squad had been there to help rescue them from the middle of an alien encampment. Theron kept a possessive arm around Sienna, who looked cute as hell in a red dress with spots on it. They had a glow about them that said they'd done more than shower after getting back from their mission.

And then there she was.

Cam stepped into the room, looking around.

Holy fuck. What the fuck was she wearing? Hemi's hands tightened on his beer. She was wearing a black dress, but there was nothing simple about it. The hemline was short, showcasing her absolutely fabulous legs. On top of that, the neckline dipped low in front, practically to her waist, and was covered in some sort of silver beads that shimmered in the light.

It was too easy to imagine his hand bunching up that tiny skirt and wrapping those long legs of hers around his hips.

He took another sip of his drink.

Hell yeah, tonight she was his.

Chapter Two

Cam shimmied her hips on the dance floor, arms raised above her head, and bumped up against Taylor. Her friend bumped her hip back against Cam and laughed.

Bringing her glass to her lips, Cam sipped her fruity frou-frou drink. She preferred beer, but it was a party, and Sienna had shoved this in her hand.

Nothing was better than blowing off steam after a mission. She studied the crowd around her. Enclave residents—young and old—were all smiling, laughing, and having fun. She saw a gray-haired couple boogie across the dance floor to a chorus of cheers. A teen boy was flexing his flirting skills on two giggling girls. A man with a sleeping toddler on his shoulder danced with a woman.

Hope. The room was filled with it. It was the one thing that they couldn't afford to lose. Cam knew from experience that once you lost hope, everything else withered, died, and turned ugly. It was worth fighting for until their last breaths.

Pushing the unhappy thoughts away, she turned her back against Taylor, and they ground against each other. Cam swung her arms, watching the light glitter off the mass of silver bracelets on her wrists.

She and Taylor moved across the dance floor. She could see Taylor searching for her man. The suave and sexy Devlin was deep in conversation with Hell Squad's scarred leader, Marcus Steele, and Niko and Roth. They all had serious expressions on their faces.

Shaking her head, Cam danced closer. "Hey, this is a party. We're supposed to be celebrating."

She knew that midnight was rapidly approaching. She fought the urge to look around and find a certain annoying berserker. Days ago, in the middle of a firefight, Hemi had claimed a midnight kiss with her. But she hadn't seen him since she'd arrived. Her lips tried to tip into a frown but she ruthlessly smiled. She was happy the idiot was staying away. If he got near her, she'd be blasting him about her helmet, not kissing him.

Roth lifted his beer. "I was filling them in on that strange area we saw."

"So, these holes in the ground...?" Niko said. "Did they look bored out? Deliberately made?"

Roth shook his head. "No. They looked more irregular and organic than that."

"No alien talk tonight." Cam cocked a hip. "Even badasses need a break. I'm calling in reinforcements." She waved at their women, and saw Avery, Taylor, Elle, and Mac head in their direction.

"Sneaky," Roth muttered. Not that he looked too upset as his gaze settled on Avery.

"The aliens aren't going anywhere for one evening," Cam said.

The women arrived, and the talk drifted away from the aliens. More drinks were poured, and soon, Elle had them in stitches over the latest one-upmanship battle between Hell Squad's sniper Shaw and his woman, Claudia.

Roth looked at his watch. "It's nearly midnight." He yanked Avery into his lap. Nearby, Taylor and Devlin were slow dancing.

Cam turned, and spotted Mac and Niko pressed against each other, the man whispering something in Mac's ear. She couldn't see Sienna and Theron, and guessed they'd snuck out to do something very naughty somewhere else.

She felt a pang of envy. She knew good relationships existed, and was so happy for her friends, but she knew it wasn't for her.

She set her shoulders back. "All these loved-up couples are giving me a toothache." She scanned the room. "I need to find a midnight kiss." She could still welcome in the New Year properly.

There were a group of people dancing nearby, but no one caught her fancy. There had been a cute, nerdy guy from the tech team who'd tripped over himself the other day, just talking to her. She searched for his name. Edward? No...Eric, that was it. He was sexy, in a geeky, shy way.

She moved over toward the food tables, looking for the tech team. She had a hunch most of them wouldn't be dancing. Sure enough, they were seated, huddled in a group. Eric was talking with another man, and a blonde woman from the tech team named Marin. The woman was super-smart, and helping with work on nullifying the alien mind-control device they'd come up against.

Marin was wearing her usual jeans and shirt. The woman was gorgeous, with blonde curls and a pretty face, but it seemed she didn't do anything to highlight her prettiness. Cam smelled a story there, somewhere. But hell, most survivors had a story or two they kept buried.

Cam set her drink down, and sauntered in Eric's direction. When he saw her coming, his eyes widened behind his glasses and he bobbled his drink. Yep, geeky cute.

She was halfway there when she felt the hairs on the back of her neck rise. She looked over her shoulder.

A big man was powering through the crowd in her direction.

Hemi always moved like a bulldozer. He wasn't the tallest of his squad, but his shoulders and chest were wide, and all muscle. He was built for power and combat.

His dark gaze locked on her, his intent clear.

"Nearly time for the countdown," a voice boomed over a loudspeaker. Cheers erupted from the crowd.

No, no, no. Cam turned quickly, and pushed her way through the cheering throng.

"Ten!" the crowd cried.

Hemi was too big, too bossy, and too alpha male. Not to mention, too annoying. She wanted nothing to do with the man.

"Nine!"

She glanced back, and couldn't see him anymore. She sucked in a deep breath. Good.

When she turned back, she saw him step in front of her.

"Eight!"

"I've not forgiven you for the rhinestones, Rahia. You do not want to be near me right now." She sidestepped and made a beeline toward Eric.

"Seven!"

"Got a kiss to claim, Cam."

His deep voice sent shivers through her body.

"Six!"

Grimly, she focused on Eric. "Hey there, handsome. I'm looking for a midnight kiss."

"Five!"

Eric's eyes bugged out of his head, and even in the darkened room, she saw the stain of a blush on his cheeks.

"Oh, well, aah..." Then, his gaze moved over her shoulder, and the color drained from his face.

"Four!"

A big hand settled on her hip, spinning her around. Her pulse spiked.

"Three!"

"Back off, Hemi."

Hard arms wrapped around her, dragging her up against a rock-hard chest.

"Time to stop running," he growled.

"Two!"

His head lowered, his lips a breath away from hers. She felt traitorous heat curling in her belly.

"What do you want, Cam?"

"One!"

She thumped a fist against his shoulder. It was like hitting rock. Damn, the scent of him wrapped around her. No cologne for Hemi—just heat and man.

"Happy New Year!"

She barely noticed the crowd cheering around her, confetti dropping from the ceiling. Her gaze locked with Hemi's, and he smiled. The man had such a disarming smile.

And beautifully formed lips surrounded by that sexy, dark beard.

She slid her hands behind his neck and yanked him down. Their lips crashed together, and in the next instant, he was kissing her.

God. God. Cam kissed him back.

***

Hell. Hemi slid his hands down, cupping Cam's ass, and pulled her closer.

She tasted so good. He slid his tongue along hers and she met him. As he'd guessed, she wasn't a passive, gentle kisser. As much as he gave, she returned it, her fingers tugging in his hair.

Hungry. He was so damn hungry for her, and so fucking turned on. He lifted his mouth. "Cam."

The crowd had exploded around them. There was cheering, whistles, and cries of "Happy New Year."

They stared at each other. He waited for her to

pull back and run...like she always did.

Then he realized her dark eyes were glazed, and filled with a hot look.

Suddenly, she leaped up and wrapped her legs around his hips. He took a step back, sliding his arms around her. Then her mouth was back on his.

Damn. He spun and headed toward the door, heedless of the people scrambling out of their way. He charged out of the packed room and into the corridor. Then, he pushed Cam up against the wall, trying to get more of her, to kiss her deeper.

"Cam." It was a barely intelligible growl.

Her mouth slid from his, her teeth dragging below his ear. "No talking." Her lips came back to his, kissing him hard.

He felt the edge of her teeth.

"My room's closer," she panted, nipping his ear.

Hell, yeah. An urgent intensity filled him. *His. Claim. Mate.* He felt like he'd been reduced to nothing more than a fucking caveman.

He spun and headed down the corridor, his hands tight on her. Cam was a tall, fit woman, but he carried her with ease. And he knew exactly where her room was.

They arrived at her door, and while he was still holding her and kissing her, she reached out behind her, slapping at the electronic lock. It took her a few tries, and a couple of moans, before she hit it correctly and the door opened.

Hemi moved inside the darkened room. She'd left a lamp on beside her bed, which diluted the shadows a little. He set her down, and felt his cock throbbing against his zipper.

He looked around, interested in seeing her space. It was messy as hell. Clothes were piled on top of chairs, and lots of stuff was scattered across her table.

Cam stepped back, her hands on her hips, which hiked that ridiculously short dress up another inch. His gaze slid down her toned legs.

"Well, Rahia?" Her voice was huskier than usual. "What now?"

There was a challenge in her voice. She was always challenging him. He closed the distance between them, then fingered the strap of her dress.

"I want you naked."

Her lips parted.

"I want that skimpy excuse for a dress off you." Yeah, his inner caveman hated knowing other men had seen those long legs, and small, high breasts. That they'd pictured being the one to touch her.

"I love this dress."

"I like your smooth, dark skin better." He stroked his hand down her collarbone. She stepped back, watching him, then slipped her fingers under the straps. She dropped them off her shoulders and the top slid down to her waist.

Holy mother of God. She wasn't wearing a bra. He stared at her breasts—small, perfect handfuls, topped with dark nipples ripe for his hungry mouth.

Then she bent over, doing a sexy little striptease, and unzipped the dress. When she stood, the fabric slithered down her body.

"Fuck." He knew his tone was reverent. She was only wearing a tiny, little, silver thong.

Her eyes glittered. "Now what?"

He tore open the buttons on his shirt and left it open. "Now I'm going to suck your nipples. Then I'm going to eat you until you scream my name."

He saw her chest hitch and he cupped her breasts. He loved seeing his big, rough hands against her smooth skin. He wrapped one arm around her slim torso, bending her back over his arm so he could suck one tight nipple into his mouth.

"Oh." Her hands tangled in his hair, holding his head to her.

He slid his other hand down the long line of her body, following the curve of her ass. He flicked at the little string that disappeared between her buttocks.

"Who did you wear this for?" He knew she sure as hell hadn't worn it for the tongue-tied tech geek. Hemi tugged on the thong.

She moaned. "Me."

"Who?"

"Me, Rahia. I don't dress for a man."

He gripped the silvery wisp of underwear, then tore it off her. Her gasp was sharp.

An overstuffed couch sat right beside them. He dropped back onto it, twisted, and stretched out on his back. "Now get up here. I want your legs wrapped around my head, and that sweet pussy of yours on my mouth and beard."

Her mouth dropped open.

He grinned. "Come on, Cam. It'll be a ride you won't forget."

She put one knee on the couch, and the way her gaze stayed on him, made him think of a lioness on the hunt. She knelt beside him and he circled her thighs with his hand and helped her up.

Fuck. She was so wet and smelled so good.

"Spread," he ordered.

She did, straddling his face with those strong thighs. He went straight for her clit. She cried out.

"Dreamed of this," he growled against her. "What you'd taste like. The sounds you'd make."

He sucked and licked, knew his beard would be rubbing some sensitive places. She cried out and shifted restlessly. Her hands sank into his hair, pulling roughly.

The husky cries she made had his throbbing cock in agony. "Grab the back of the couch."

She released his hair and gripped the couch, fingers sinking into the cushions. He grabbed one of her thighs, pushing it wider to give him better access. He lapped at her, hard and unforgiving, and she ground against his mouth, her cries becoming more urgent, her body rocking.

Then she tensed, her legs tightening around him. Her head flew back and her body shook as she came with a scream.

"Hemi!"

He held her there for a second, savoring the sexy taste of her, before he helped her flop on top of him. She threw an arm over her flushed face.

"You have a clever tongue," she said lazily.

He flicked at one nipple again and it puckered instantly. "Who did you wear the lace for?"

"No one."

"Who were you imagining taking it off? Who'd you imagine touching and tasting you, and making you come?"

She shot him a haughty look. "I'm perfectly capable of giving myself a good orgasm."

"But it's not the same as a man worshiping you." He nipped her shoulder. "Not the same as his tongue on you, or his cock moving inside you."

"Hemi—"

"Who? Whose hands did you want?"

"Hemi. Let's not—"

He nipped the curve of her breast this time. "Who, Cam?"

"Dammit, you." Her hand wrapped around his wrist. "I wanted you."

Wild satisfaction flooded him, and he slammed his mouth down on hers.

Chapter Three

Damn, Hemi Rahia was in her room. And worse than that, she was having sex with Hemi Rahia. Hot, wild, delicious sex.

He slid a hand down her body, finding all her sensitive places. The man had big, rough hands. Cam liked them.

And that beard and mouth…she was still tingling between her thighs.

It had been too long since she'd had a man naked. So Hemi was breaking her drought. She'd get him out of her system and then send him on his way. What she wouldn't do was let him stamp himself all over her personal quarters, her little sanctuary. And he was absolutely not allowed in her bed…that was far too intimate.

He was touching her again, callused fingers running over her skin. Dammit, she was trembling.

It didn't matter how good he felt, how good he made her feel, she didn't need to smell him on her sheets. She didn't want the memories.

"I need you inside me." She slid her hand down, caressing hard muscles. God, every inch of him was muscle on muscle. Built for power. He still had his shirt on, but with it open, she had a good view of some of the incredible Maori-style tattoos, etched in black ink on his dark-bronze skin. She traced them with her fingers.

She needed him inside her. Just so she could work the tattooed troublemaker out of her system.

She shifted, straddling his body. "Right here." She let her hand drift down to toy with the zipper on his jeans. There was a large, very hard bulge beneath the denim.

Damn, there was a lot of him. She palmed him and he groaned.

Cam flicked open the top of his trousers. "What do you have in here for me, Rahia?"

She pulled out a very thick cock. *Oh boy*. She stroked him. "Fuck me."

"I'm going to. Hard." His voice was a growl. "On the bed."

Her pulse leaped. "We have a perfectly good couch right here."

He grabbed her wrist, pushing her to her feet. "Bed."

Panic trickled through Cam. She looked around, and her gaze fell on the brand-new armchair that she'd just finished reupholstering. "Why not christen my newest acquisition?" She nodded toward the big chair. She'd covered it in a lovely blue fabric, and it was huge with large arms. She'd planned to while the hours away in it, listening to music or reading a book.

She pulled away from Hemi, and sauntered over to the chair. She knew she had a good body. Far too many times, pre-invasion, she'd been approached by modeling scouts. Walking a runway sounded mind-numbingly boring to her, but she wasn't above using what she'd been born with when it suited her.

Especially when she was wearing nothing but her sparkly, silver, high-heeled shoes.

She put her hands down on the arms of the chair, and arched her back. She looked over her shoulder.

His gaze was glued to her ass.

"What are you waiting for?"

He was on her in an instant, hands palming her cheeks. She felt his fingers slide between her thighs and she moaned. One thick finger thrust inside her.

"So wet, Cam. You're ready for my cock."

She pushed back against him and moaned. She couldn't control her reaction.

He slid a second finger inside her. "You're tight, baby. You'll feel me when I stretch you."

She'd always known that being with Hemi would be a little bit dirty. Then, his fingers were gone. She made a small, mewling cry.

He picked her up around her waist. "Now, on the bed."

"No." She hit the covers and bounced once.

He loomed beside the bed, stripping off his clothes with hard, yanking movements.

"I want to christen my new chair."

"Bed."

Cam stilled. *Holy hell.* All she saw were sharply etched muscles and tattoos. There was no color, only black ink in the designs that made her think of island warriors.

He put one knee on the bed, his gaze intent on her.

"I thought you'd be more creative," she said with a sniff.

"You got a problem with the bed? Got a problem knowing we're going to spend the rest of the night in it?"

Her heart squeezed and she tried to sound normal. "Hemi—"

"You are so fucking beautiful, Cam."

She'd heard it before. It didn't mean much. She'd been born like this, she hadn't earned it or worked for it. His big hands circled her ankles and stroked up her legs.

"You're so strong and tough." He pushed her legs apart. "I want you to watch me slide inside you."

She was panting now, watching as his big body moved between her spread legs. His caresses were so bold and rough against her skin. Like he owned her.

Okay, so he was in her bed. They'd have some fun, work out this tension between them. But he wasn't sleeping here. Once he was done, he'd leave, and that would be that.

She watched, as he circled his thick cock, and all thoughts flew from her head. She looked down, her chest heaving, and watched as he rubbed the head of his cock through her folds.

God. She arched her back.

"Do you have a functioning contraceptive

implant?" His voice was a low growl.

"Yes." That thick, hard cock looked brutish against her smoothness.

"Watch." A guttural demand.

Slowly, ever so slowly, he pushed inside her.

She'd expected fast, hard, rough. Instead, she got a slow, steady claiming that stretched her to the limit and fired every nerve ending. *So thick.* She cried out. Hemi Rahia was inside her, and it was too much.

***

Hemi was in his own personal heaven. It didn't matter what happened to him from now on, he'd die happy.

He thrust inside Cam's warm tightness. Jesus, the noises she made... He felt her muscles clamping down on him, and he plunged wildly.

"Yes," she cried. "Yes."

"Been waiting so long for this." He kept his strokes hard and solid. He reached up and linked the fingers of his left hand with hers. "Been waiting my whole fucking life."

Hemi had no control, no restraint. He heard the bed frame smacking against the wall, punctuated by Cam's cries.

He saw her head had fallen back, showcasing the slim, perfect form of her torso and long neck.

"Cam." His voice was low and rough. "Look at me."

Brown eyes opened, her gaze hot.

"You keep your eyes on mine." He wanted to watch everything that crossed her face.

He thrust deeper and her lips parted.

"You like that? You like me inside you?"

"Yes."

Hemi could barely think, only heard the roar of his heartbeat in his ears. There was only Cam, the feel of her, and the pleasure growing in him—raw and primal.

He saw her chest hitch, felt her body clamp down on his. Yes. "Come, baby."

She came with a wild cry. He drove inside her again and again.

Dazed eyes drifted lower, over his body, down to where he was moving inside her.

"Again," he demanded.

Her eyes widened. "I can't."

He kept thrusting. He wanted to make sure Cam had no doubts about who she belonged to. He wanted to claim her, mark her as his.

Reaching down, he gripped her legs and pushed them up until her ankles rested on his shoulders. It gave him a better angle to pound inside her.

Cam reached up, her nails scraping down his biceps. She let out another guttural cry that made his cock throb, and she came again.

This time, as her body clamped down on his cock, it triggered his own release. He roared his pleasure and spilled himself inside her.

A second later, he shifted her legs and collapsed down, his body half on top of her.

"Fuck." His brain was fried. His chest heaved, as

he tried to get air into his starved lungs.

"Fuck is right," she murmured.

"Knew it would be like this."

She made a humming sound.

"Can't wait to do it again."

"No way, Rahia," she said. "This is a one-shot deal."

Hemi stiffened for a second, then he smiled. There was his little echidna, with her quills bristling. He knew she'd try to rebuild the walls between them.

Screw that. He was in now, and he wasn't letting Cam push him out again.

He rolled, tucking her close to his side. "We are going to do it again."

She blew out a breath, warm air fanning across his shoulder. "I said no."

Hemi skimmed a hand down her body and felt her tremble. "You sure?"

"I…" her voice drifted off.

He reached out and touched her nipple, tweaking it between his fingers. "Cam? You sure?"

She shivered under his touch and then she sniffed. "One more time. But that's it."

He grinned, letting his hand drift down her belly and between her thighs. "Fucking love it that you have no hair here." He took his time stroking her, thumbing her clit. Her hips arched up. "You want more Hemi, don't you, baby?"

"Don't push it, Rahia," she snapped.

Her snarky tone made his cock harden. He rubbed her clit until she was writhing against the sheets. "I want to hear you say my name when you come."

"Screw you."

"You did that already, and will again. Now, you come again, and you say my name again when you do."

"No."

He slid two fingers inside her warmth, still working her clit.

"Damn you," she said. "Remember, one more time." She was panting now. "And once we're done you're gone. I like my space, and don't want you sleeping here."

They'd see about that. "Say my name, Cam."

Without warning her, he moved up and covered her body. He slid inside her with one hard thrust. She reared up, her teeth sinking into his shoulder. When she came, she screamed his name.

Chapter Four

Cam woke and started to stretch lazily. Then she went still, and blinked. She was pinned to the mattress, a hard warmth behind her, and a massive arm draped over her waist.

It only took a microsecond to remember who was pressed against her, holding her tight.

She squeezed her eyes shut. *Dammit. Dammit. Dammit.*

One rule. Don't let him into her bed. What the hell had gotten into her? Apart from Hemi's thick and very energetic cock.

She turned her head and glanced at the clock. God, they'd only slept the last few hours. The rest of the night...well, Hemi wasn't only a bulldozer out of bed—strong and unstoppable. She put a choke hold on the sexy memories trying to push into her head.

Carefully, she slipped to the side of the bed, but before she could escape, the arm around her tightened.

"Need the bathroom," she whispered.

The arm loosened.

Cam slid out of the bed and watched as he rolled

over, taking up the small portion that she'd had.

He sprawled in abandon, and she had the perfect view of his massive, naked body. He wasn't beautiful, but the Maori tattoos covering one side of his back were. Her gaze drifted down, over his tightly muscled ass, and the strong tree trunks of thighs.

Her gut clenched. She recalled running her tongue over some of those tattoos, and her nails digging into his ass. She wanted to do it again.

No. No. No. She turned around, and snatched up some panties off a folded pile on a chair. Next, she snatched up some gym clothes off the floor. She gave them a quick sniff. They didn't smell bad. She yanked on leggings, feeling the fabric rasp over sensitized skin. Next came a sports bra and a shirt.

She desperately needed something to keep her mind off of…her gaze went back to the man in her bed. Things.

She needed to get out of there until he was gone. Then, she'd put this behind her.

Hemi might be part Neanderthal, but he was also a good guy. A guy who'd grown up with brothers and a tight family.

And Cam hadn't.

She slipped her feet into some running shoes, and then snuck out the door.

The corridors of the Enclave were quiet. Everyone was clearly sleeping off last night's party.

When she stepped into the gym, she found the place empty, and breathed a sigh of relief. She bypassed the treadmills—she detested them—and headed for an exercise bike. Soon, she'd worked up a good sweat, her legs burning from the exertion.

After a while, she abandoned the bike and headed over to lift some weights.

"I didn't expect to see you here this morning."

Cam spun and saw Sienna. "Right back at you."

"Theron had promised boxing lessons to a couple of the teens." Sienna's eyes went soft at the thought of her man working with kids. "I thought I'd climb for a bit." She nodded toward the climbing wall at the back of the gym, but then her nose wrinkled. "Work off my hangover."

Cam smiled. "I prefer working my hangover off in a dark room with a Bloody Mary."

Sienna tilted her head, her brown eyes scanning Cam's face. "You okay? Usually you avoid the gym, if you can help it. Hell, usually you avoid standing up, if you can help it."

Cam shrugged, trying to look casual. "Sure, I'm okay. Peachy. Why?" Did she look different? Did she have a brand announcing Hemi had given her six screaming orgasms?

Sienna kept staring at her. "Did you have a good night?"

"Sure. Great party. I was tired and went to bed afterward." That wasn't a lie. She'd been in her bed.

Her squad mate looked like she was fighting back a smile. "Pretty nice hickey on the side of your neck."

"What?" Cam touched her neck and hit a tender spot. Damn, Hemi. "Oh, I…scratched myself when I was getting dressed this morning."

"It's surrounded by stubble burn, if I'm not mistaken."

Shit. Cam blew out a breath. "All right, fine. I slept with Hemi."

Sienna's eyes widened. "Really?" The word came out part squeal.

"Well, okay, that's not entirely true. We didn't sleep much."

"Was it good?"

"Sienna!"

"Come on, tell me. On a scale of one to ten."

Memories hit Cam and her pulse jumped. "Like a hundred and seven."

"Wowser." Then Sienna's eyes turned dreamy. "Theron's a hundred and seven, as well."

"Enough." Cam cut a hand through the air. "I don't need images of you and Theron doing it like rabbits in my head while we're on a mission."

"So…Hemi, huh?"

"Yes. Shit." Cam dropped down on a weight bench.

"He's wanted you a long time. He'll be good for you. And under all that roughness is a great guy."

Cam shook her head. "We aren't together, Sienna."

Her friend frowned. "Oh?"

"It was a one-night deal. To get it out of our systems."

Now Sienna snorted. "I've heard that before. So, how's your system?"

Hot and bothered, and it wanted more. "My

system is fine."

"Uh-huh. And Hemi agreed to one night?"

"Well, we didn't spend a lot of time talking."

"Uh-huh."

Cam strongly disliked that smug sound. "Stop that. Look, don't say anything to anyone, okay?"

The gym door slammed open and Mac walked in. "There you guys are. Roth needs us up in ops."

Cam stood. If Roth needed them first thing on New Year's morning, something was up.

Sienna spun around. "Cam slept with Hemi."

Cam gasped. "What part of 'don't tell anyone' didn't you understand?"

Mac's dark eyebrows rose. "About time. Was it good?"

Cam let out a short, frustrated scream, and stomped out of the gym.

***

Hemi opened his eyes and stretched out an arm. The bed was empty and he was alone.

He muttered a curse and rolled onto his back. Of course, he was. Cam had done what Cam did best—run. What else had he expected?

He scrunched a pillow up under his head, and breathed deep. It smelled of her.

It didn't take much for him to remember all the things they'd done to each other in her bed. All the ways he'd touched her, all that sexy passion, the way she'd called out his name. Hell, she was hot. She'd singed his skin, and as he'd always known it would be, sliding into her had been the best thing he'd done.

He smiled to himself. He'd won the battle. He'd keep up his assault until he won the war.

The comm unit beside the bed chimed and he hit the button without thinking. "Yeah."

"Need you in ops." It was Tane's deep voice.

"How did you know I was here?" Hemi asked.

Silence.

Right. His brother was spooky-good at finding people. Had been, even as a kid. Although, if Tane had seen him kissing Cam last night, it probably hadn't taken much for him to work out where Hemi was.

Hemi sat up with a flex of his abdomen. "I'll be there."

He rolled out of bed and pulled his clothes on. He didn't have time to head to his room to change. He cast one more glance at Cam's bed, with its twisted sheets, then headed in the direction of the Command Center.

When he stepped inside, he found the room packed with his squad members, along with Hell Squad and Squad Nine. Something was definitely up.

His gaze zeroed in on Cam. She was wearing workout gear, and was studiously avoiding him. Damn, she looked edible. He let himself take in all the long lines of her, while imagining just what was beneath the fabric.

Need slammed into him and his fingers curled into a fist. It was so much worse now that he knew

41

exactly what being with her was like.

"Someone's still wearing last night's clothes," an amused voice drawled.

Hemi glanced over at Ash. The man was grinning at him, tattooed arms crossed over his chest.

"Got lucky?" Levi was grinning, too, his hair pulled up in a messy knot.

Hemi was feeling too good to let them bait him. He pulled out a chair and sat down. "Yeah."

"Was it good?" Levi waggled his eyebrows.

"Best night of my life." He wanted to look at Cam, but he avoided it. If he caused messy gossip, she'd skewer him. He might enjoy it, but he wouldn't put something private out there until she was ready.

He felt his squad mates looking at him with keen interest. Man, they were the worst gossips sometimes.

"Thank you all for coming." The authoritative voice of General Adam Holmes cut across the room. The general moved to the front of the crowd, wearing a neatly-pressed uniform. He was backlit by the wall of the screens. "I'm afraid your first day of the New Year will be spent planning a mission."

"What's up?" Marcus asked in his gravelly voice.

"The tech team has been working with the medical team to study the new creeper alien that Theron and Sienna identified on the last mission."

An image flashed up on the screen of the new alien. It was big, with six legs and an orange belly. Not to mention the ugly sucker mouth it used to eat living things whole. It looked like a mutated spider gone horribly wrong.

"Hell Squad brought back a creeper carcass from the power station mission," Holmes continued.

That mission had been to rescue Theron and Sienna. The Squad Nine pair had gotten themselves stuck on an alien ship that landed in an alien encampment outside a hydro-electric power station several hours south of the Enclave.

Hemi grinned and caught Tane's gaze. They'd made a hell of a mess for the aliens to clean up during that rescue.

"It looks like these creatures swallow a living being, and store it in their stomach. That's where it's transformed into some sort of Gizzida hybrid. The stomach eventually detaches as a pod." The general's brow was furrowed. "Doc Emerson thinks that if the pod is left undisturbed to final maturation, the change to full Gizzida would be complete."

"So, no more need for genesis tanks," Roth muttered.

There were frustrated rumbles all around the room. All of them knew about the aliens' tanks. Filled with alien liquid, humans were forced into them, floating there for months, until they turned into aliens.

But now it appeared these creepers were the new version.

"That's all we know for now," Holmes said. "We don't know how long the transformation takes, or how to neutralize them."

Shit. Hemi stretched his legs out in front of him. Not good.

Holmes shoved his hands in his pockets. "Noah and Emerson have informed me that they would learn more if we had a live creeper."

What? Hemi sat up. Noah was head of the tech team, and Emerson the lead doctor who patched them all up. He glanced around and saw that no one looked happy. He traded a look with Tane, and his brother shook his head.

"You want to bring a live alien creature into the Enclave?" Marcus said in a measured tone.

"We held alien prisoners at Blue Mountain Base," Holmes said.

"Not ones that ate people whole," Roth countered.

A woman stepped up beside the general. Her red hair was pulled back in a neat braid, and her bearing was straight. "My team is working on containment for the creature."

Captain Laura Bladon was head of the interrogation team, and ran the prison cells. Back at Blue Mountain Base, before it had been destroyed, she'd held and interrogated a number of raptors.

"Gaz'da has been helping and providing invaluable information," she said. "We are building cages out on the edge of the Enclave. We're also ensuring we have security protocols in place, so that if the alien creeper escapes, it can't reach the main part of the base."

Gaz'da was a raptor that had been a prisoner at

Blue Mountain Base. He'd turned on the Gizzida who'd forcibly changed him and was helping Laura. Hemi wasn't sure how he felt about a raptor being resident at the Enclave, but Gaz'da stayed in the prison area, worked with Laura and her team, and appeared to be a valuable asset.

"So." Holmes' blue gaze ran over them all. "I need a team to head back to the power station encampment, and capture a creeper."

"How the hell are we supposed to do that?" Roth asked.

"And how the hell do we bring it back here?" Tane added.

"Doc Emerson has concocted some powerful sedatives. She believes they will keep the creeper knocked out for transport."

"Believes?" Tane asked.

Holmes gave an unhappy nod. "It's the best we can do."

Laura clasped her hands behind her back. "We have stunner prods and nets that my team have used and modified. They'll be helpful for catching the creature."

"I want volunteers," the general said. "A mix from Squad Nine, Squad Three and Hell Squad to make up a team. Four in total." His gaze swung to Roth.

"Cam's up next for a joint mission," Roth said.

Cam nodded.

Hemi glanced at Tane. If Cam was going, he was sure as fuck going, too.

Tane stepped forward. "Hemi."

Cam's head whipped around, and their eyes met. *Yeah, that's right, baby. Not letting you head into alien territory on your own.*

"Can the sedatives be administered by rifle shot?" Marcus asked.

"Yes," Holmes answered.

"Then you'll need Shaw."

Shaw Baird was the best sniper in the base.

"And I want to go to round out the team," Claudia Frost said.

Holmes nodded. "Very well. Plan your mission. See Laura and Emerson for the equipment you'll need. And good luck."

Chapter Five

Cam strode into the small conference room that they were using for their planning meeting. She'd timed her arrival a little late, hoping that everyone would be there. But when she entered, she only saw Hemi sprawled in a chair.

Great. She stopped in her tracks.

"Hello, Camryn," he drawled.

She studied his face and couldn't judge his mood. When her gaze dropped to his lips, and memories threatened, she looked away. "Hemi. Shaw and Claudia not here yet?"

"On their way."

Searching for something to do, she walked over to the large screen on the wall, and tapped on the surface. She started pulling up the maps they'd need for planning.

"You had to race off to work out this morning?" His voice was a deep rumble.

She sniffed, hating that she heard a hint of disappointment in his voice. "Things to do."

"You want to pretend last night didn't happen?"

He didn't seem bothered by that idea. She felt a sharp sting of unfamiliar pain. That was what she wanted. Absolutely. But was it that easy for him to brush away their night together?

She spun and lifted her chin. "Sure." She strode past him, heading for a chair.

A strong arm reached out, and the next thing she knew, she was yanked into his lap.

"Hey!"

He gripped her chin, his calluses rasping on her skin. His gaze hit her hickey, and she saw male satisfaction slide through his eyes.

"Not gonna happen," he said.

"What?"

"I'm not going to forget I was inside you. Not going to forget you rode my mouth and beard. Not going to forget you screamed my name." He pulled her close, until their noses brushed. "In fact, I'm going to relive every memory in great detail."

"Hemi—" She slammed her hands against his hard chest. He was too big, too hot, too much.

"I'm going to fuck you again. And again. Until I don't wake up alone and find you gone. Until I wake up with you in my arms."

"One night. That was it!"

"It's gonna happen again. I want to do you from behind. I want to watch you suck my cock. I want to put my mouth between your legs again and make you feel good."

Cam felt that traitorous rush of heat between her thighs. Then, he leaned closer and kissed her.

She fought...for about two seconds. But he tasted so good, felt so good. She tangled her tongue with his, her hands sliding up to tangle in his hair. He'd worn it long when she'd first met him, but had recently cut it a little shorter and shaved it at the sides. She'd never admit it, but she liked it.

His fingers brushed down her neck, fingering the tender skin of her hickey. He lifted his lips from hers. "I like knowing I marked you."

"Neanderthal," she muttered.

"You marked me, too." His grin was wide. "I have some pretty spectacular scratch marks down my back and on my ass."

Cam sniffed. *Dammit.* She wanted to see them.

He moved and set her on her feet. "For now, we have a mission to plan, but Cam—" His dark eyes were intense and liquid. "I'm going to run you down. You're fast, but I have stamina."

Infuriating man. She set her hands on her hips. "Hemi, let's just keep this fun, okay?" She could do fun. It was everything else that freaked her out.

"Oh, we'll have fun, but that's not all we'll have."

She opened her mouth to argue, but at that moment the door opened.

"You feel me up in the Command Center again, Baird, and I'll break your arm." Claudia's sharp voice.

"There's my badass girl. If you break my arm, how will I bring you your coffee in bed in the morning? Or touch you in all those secret places you love—" Shaw spotted Hemi and Cam and broke off with a wide smile. "Howdy."

"Shaw." Hemi didn't bother hiding his grin.

Claudia swept in. "So, you guys ready to hunt and capture an alien creeper? And not let it eat you in the process?"

"Hell yeah," Hemi replied.

Cam sat and nodded. "Let's do it.

The next few hours turned into a mix of studying maps, suggesting and discarding ideas, and studying images of the creature. Laura arrived with a large bag filled with stunner prods and heavy-duty metal nets. She gave them all a lesson on using the prods and deploying the nets.

"These prods are our latest design," the redhead said. "They're telescoping, so you can carry them more easily, and extend them when needed."

Cam shook the prod and the end extended. She knew it would administer a high-voltage stun to the alien. She retracted it. *Nice*.

Laura gave them a perfect salute. "Good luck out there."

After Laura, Doc Emerson arrived, her white lab coat flapping behind her as she hurried in. She set a small case down on the table, and unsnapped the lid. "Hello, everyone. I'm your friendly base drug dealer."

"Too pretty to be a drug dealer," Hemi said.

She winked at him. "Oh, is there a rule that drug dealers can only be ugly?"

He barked out a laugh as the doctor lifted a vial out of her case.

"High grade, very powerful sedatives." The liquid was clear. "I've been working on these stronger sedatives for Laura's team, when I'm not busy trying to sort out the contraceptive implants." Her gaze turned distant for a second, like she was running experiments in her head.

"How's that going?" Cam asked. Her implant was nearing the end of its life. She hadn't given it much thought, since she hadn't had sex in a while, but now... She avoided looking at Hemi.

The doc nodded. "Getting there. I can squeeze a bit more time out of the current implants, but I don't have a long-term solution yet." She set the vial back in the case. "These can be put in casings you can use with a rifle." She pushed the case toward Shaw.

"Thanks." Shaw's face was serious. Cam knew the man was quick to tease and laugh, but he was also one hell of a soldier.

"Be careful out there," Emerson said, heading for the door. "If you get hurt, I'll stick you with lots of needles and confine you to bed rest."

Cam leaned back in her chair. "So, once we catch the creeper, how do we get back to the Enclave?" The damn things were too big to fit in a Hawk.

"I've been talking with Finn," Claudia said. "That's why Shaw and I were late. He thinks we can suspend the creature under a Hawk. They have cargo slings that we can use."

Hemi leaned forward with a frown. "Will it be covered by the Hawk's illusion system?"

Shaw shook his head. "Nope." He grinned. "We'll be out and proud."

Cam tried to picture what a giant creeper would look like flying through the air under a camouflaged quadcopter. "It'll make a nice target for any alien ptero ships in the vicinity."

"We'll need extra weapons on the Hawk to

defend ourselves on the ride back," Hemi suggested.

"My squad can provide an escort with the Darkswifts," Cam said. The two-man, powered gliders were fast, and equipped with laser cannons. "They can shoot down anyone who gets close to us."

"Good idea," Hemi said.

"Okay," Claudia said. "I'll coordinate with Finn. We'll leave for the power station in the morning."

As Claudia and Shaw left, Cam tried to bolt around the table and get out quickly.

Hemi grabbed the back of her shirt and pulled her toward him. *No. No. No.*

"I've got things to do, Hemi."

"I'm teaching some of the kids to play rugby. I need an assistant, and told them you'd swing by."

What? "I don't know much about rugby."

"Some of the girls were excited you'd be there."

Tricky, underhanded man. "Like I said...things to do."

"Oh?" He raised a brow. "I'll tell the kids that you had more important things to do, then."

She narrowed her gaze. "That's blackmail."

"Whatever it takes."

She barely stopped herself from growling. "I hate you."

He grinned at her. "No, you don't."

"I'm not good with kids, Hemi."

"They're kids, not raptors."

She wavered. How could she refuse to help kids?

"It'll be fun." He slung an arm across her shoulders. "And I promise not to feel you up."

"Fine. But I can't promise not to break your arm."

***

When they walked into the indoor arena, Hemi could still feel the anger radiating off Cam. Damn, she was gorgeous when she was angry. And when she was angry, she was too busy to be worried about strengthening those walls of hers. That's why he was always messing with her.

Ahead, a group of teenagers waited. "Hey, gang."

The kids surrounded them. The younger ones were all bright faces and eagerness. The older ones hung back, playing it cool. Hemi fist-bumped a few of them.

He spotted a younger boy. "Hey, Bastian."

The dark-haired boy nodded. He'd survived the invasion, and had ended up living at the Enclave without his parents. After meeting up with Roth, the boy had been reunited with his parents at Blue Mountain Base before making the trip back to the Enclave. Hemi was sure as hell glad to see some families had had happy reunions. The same couldn't be said for most.

"Can't wait to play today." Bastian's gaze slid to Cam and his cheeks pinkened. "Hi, Cam."

"Hi, B."

Hemi hid a smile. Looked like the kid had a major crush. Couldn't blame him. Cam looked good in her skin-hugging workout gear—strong, sleek, and beautiful.

"All right, you lazy gits." He clapped his hands together. "Let's play. I need you to split into two teams."

Cam moved forward, helping some of the youngest split off into the teams, ensuring an even match of younger and older kids.

Hemi paired them off and got them passing and kicking to each other to warm up.

He grabbed a rugby ball, spinning it in his hands. He'd been playing rugby since he could walk. It was in his blood. His older brother Manu had played for the United Coalition National team for a few years, and a couple of his cousins had been on league teams before the invasion.

A hard sensation filled his chest. They were probably dead now. His thoughts turned to his sprawling family. He prayed his Ma and Pa were okay. They had a house on acreage outside of Christchurch, on New Zealand's South Island. Pa was ex-military, and his Ma was tough as they came. They could have survived.

"Hemi?"

He turned his head and saw Cam watching him.

"You okay?" she asked.

He nodded. "Fine. Time to play." He glanced at the kids. "Leo, you're captain of your team. Maria, you're captain of the other."

Hemi called out a reminder of the rules. He'd been working with the kids for a few weeks now, and they were getting the hang of it. He focused on their fresh, smiling faces. They were alive, and they needed things like sports to give them some sense of normality and help them cope.

He tossed the ball at Leo. "Remember, keep those tackles below the neck. Let's play."

The game started. Hemi kept an eye on them, making sure no one got tackled too hard. He acted as referee, making the calls. He got a few grumbles and muttered curses, but a hard stare usually kept the complainers in line. The rest of the time was filled with laughter and good-natured teasing. He called out advice for the scrums and offered a few passing tips.

One boy bowed out. "Think I pulled a muscle in my thigh."

Cam helped the boy, Luke, to a bench. Hemi checked him over. "That hurt?"

"Not too much."

"Think we can avoid Medical. Rest it."

"We're short one player," Leo said. The older teen's eyes landed on Cam. "Looks like you'll have to play, Cam."

She raised a brow. "What?"

Leo grabbed her hand and yanked her onto the field. "You don't want to disappoint the kids, do you?"

She eyed the boy. "Have you been taking blackmail lessons from Hemi?"

She put up a token protest, but soon she was in line with the rest of the team. Hemi blew his whistle.

Cam laughed as she passed the ball to her teammates. And was laughing again when she got tackled. God, he loved her laugh. Carefree and sexy, all rolled into one.

Clare, Leo's girlfriend, limped off the field, her face damp with sweat. She was on the opposing team. "I need a break, Hemi." She handed him the ball with a smile. "Why don't you take over for me?"

Hemi grinned and handed her his whistle. He fell into line with his team, facing off against Cam's. His gaze caught hers, and he saw that familiar glint of challenge.

The whistle blew. Hemi got the ball, and powered down the field toward the goal posts. He was tackled by not one, but two teens. They all fell on the synthetic grass in a tangle of limbs and laughter.

"Hey, both of you can't tackle me at once," he complained.

"One of us would never get you down," a pretty, young blonde girl said. "You're huge."

"Sounds fair to me," Cam called out.

On the next charge, Cam had the ball, sprinting toward the goal, dodging her opponents. She dived gracefully over the line and scored. She got up and did a victory dance. Her team rushed up to her and gave her high-fives.

"Oh, yeah. Take that, Rahia." She sent him a saucy look.

He crossed his arms over his chest. He loved seeing her so happy and relaxed. Something told him that Cam hadn't had much of that when she'd been the same age as these kids. "Bet you can't do it again."

"Oh?" She cocked her hip. Around them, the kids

started cheering and egging them on.

"I bet I can."

"Can't."

Her gaze narrowed. "I can and when I do, you'll owe me."

"What?"

She tapped her chin. "Whatever I want."

"You're on. The same if I win."

She hesitated a second, but the kids' cheers grew louder. She waved at them. "Let's do this."

They lined up again.

Clare blew the whistle. "Go!"

Leo ran and passed the ball. The next kid fumbled the ball, but managed to get it to Cam. She ran, sprinting down the field as fast as she could.

Hemi spun and gave chase. He ran very fast in a straight line. He tackled her, spinning them in midair, and they went down. He took the brunt of the fall, before he rolled on top of her. She was panting, her chest moving against his.

"Damn." She was flushed and smiling.

He dropped his forehead to hers. "I really want to kiss you." He kept his voice low and tried to not let himself forget the room full of kids.

"So," Cam said. "What are you going to claim as your prize?"

He shifted, pressing his lips to her neck, right over the mark he'd left on her skin. "I know what I want."

Her tone turned wary. "What's that?"

"Your lips wrapped around my—"

She shoved hard against his chest. "I think I get the picture, Rahia. Now off."

With a laugh, he leaped to his feet and pulled her up. "Okay, drinks are on me," he called out.

The kids cheered. While they'd been playing, he'd arranged for the kitchen staff to bring drinks and snacks. The kids fell on the loaded table like starving locusts.

Hemi snagged a chocolate chip cookie and handed it to Cam. He knew that she loved them. She stared at it for a second, before she snatched it and took a bite.

As he grabbed a drink of cold water, he watched the kids around him, laughing. Clare was hugging a smaller girl, and a few others were recapping their favorite moments of the game.

"They make wading through the muck worthwhile, don't they?" Cam said quietly.

"Yeah, they do," he agreed. "Family makes it worthwhile." And a woman who was worth it made it damn worthwhile, too.

"You're pretty comfy being surrounded by kids." She eyed him. "For a badass former mercenary."

"I came from a big family. Every Sunday, we had lunch at our house. My Ma cooked way too much food and my aunts, uncles and cousins would arrive. We'd crowd around the table and then head outside to throw a rugby ball around. You should have seen our holidays."

She cocked her head. "You miss them."

"Every damn day." He took a swig of his drink. "What about your family?"

She went stiff and then shrugged. "I'm an only child. No rugby games at my place."

When she didn't say anything else, he moved closer. "Your parents?"

"My mom was in Kenya visiting her family when the invasion happened." All the warmth had gone out of Cam's voice. "My father was Scottish, and traveled a lot for work. I've no idea where he was. I don't know if they made it."

He hated hearing her blank tone. Cam was always full of life and laughter. "You want to talk about it?"

"No."

He wouldn't push her. Instead, he touched the back of her neck and squeezed.

She closed her eyes. "Don't be sweet."

"Harder for you to push me away and run from me when I'm being sweet."

She turned away, knocking his hand off her. "I'm quick, Rahia. And you aren't that sweet, so don't get cocky." She started to saunter away.

Hemi snatched up a cookie and watched her, unconcerned. "Remember, you owe me my prize." They weren't done yet.

She shot him one fulminating look as she left.

Chapter Six

Cam fastened the last of her armor around her torso. She touched the button that sent her combat helmet sliding into place, then retracted it again. She'd managed to pry most of the rhinestones off, with some help from a bad-smelling chemical she'd gotten from the tech team. She lifted her carbine and checked her weapon.

She was ready for the mission. She would have liked a little more sleep, but dreams of a certain tattoo-covered annoyance had disturbed her slumber.

She heaved up the bag at her feet—filled with the stunner prods and nets. The damn thing was heavy, but the exoskeleton built into her armor made it easy enough for her to lift.

After taking a deep breath, she headed out of her squad locker room.

Her squad was waiting in the corridor.

"Ready?" Roth asked.

She fought back a smile. "As ready as I'll ever be."

"You'll be out of drone coverage near the alien encampment, but once you catch the creeper, you head north until you can contact us again."

"Yes, Dad."

"Be careful out there," Sienna said.

"And kick some alien butt," Taylor added.

Mac and Theron gave her silent nods.

Her friends hugged her and slapped her on the back.

"Okay, I have a Hawk to catch." She hitched the bag up. "I'll be back with an ugly creeper in tow."

Cam headed toward the Hawk hangar. In her head, she ran over all the mission parameters.

"I'll take that." A big hand grabbed the handle of the bag.

She looked over her shoulder and saw the man responsible for her disrupted sleep. Her pulse spiked. "I've got it."

"I'll carry it."

She yanked the bag closer. He tried to pull it away. They got into a tug-of-war.

"I'm wearing my armor," she said. "I can carry it."

Hemi yanked again and managed to pull it away from her. He gave her a satisfied grin.

She shook her head. "Fine. Carry it, then."

She stomped the rest of the way to the hangar. Inside, maintenance crew members were circling the quadcopters, performing pre-flight checks. Cam spotted Claudia, also armored up, standing near one Hawk in the center of the space.

The female soldier was holding the case of sedatives. When she saw Cam and Hemi, she tossed them a salute.

Suddenly, a blond head popped out of the open

side door of the Hawk. "Ready to capture a creepy alien incubator?" Finn called out.

"Great pep talk, Erickson," Hemi said.

The Hawk pilot looked unrepentant. "Only the best of service with Erickson Air."

"We going or what?" Shaw's voice from inside the Hawk. The sniper appeared, cradling a rifle. It wasn't his usual long-range laser weapon. This one was made for firing the sedatives.

Soon they were all aboard and strapped in. The Hawk took off, flying vertically, rock walls visible through the side windows before they cleared the retracted hangar doors. The Hawk rotated, and they flew south.

They had all been in this position so many times before. That hushed moment before a mission, adrenaline building, thoughts churning. Right now, Cam ran through every step of the mission, conscious of that tiny seed in the back of her mind that whispered that maybe this time she wouldn't make it home. And the other thought...that reminded her that she was doing it for a good reason.

Cam glanced over and saw Hemi, sprawled in his chair, eyes closed and looking relaxed.

Instantly, her mind showered her in memories. The things they'd done in her bed, him sliding inside her, moving thickly.

No. No. No. She wasn't thinking about that.

And she certainly wasn't thinking about the "prize" she owed him.

Claudia handed out the stunner prods, and Cam

clipped hers onto her belt. Hemi and Claudia stashed the nets in smaller backpacks.

"Approaching mission area," Finn called back.

The energy in the Hawk changed, sharpened. Cam rose and looked out the small side window. A long, narrow valley lay nestled in the Snowy Mountains. She saw a lake, and in the distance, the large white pipes of the hydro-electric power station, running over the hills like giant snakes. She knew that near the large, squat building at the base of the pipes, the aliens had amassed and were planning...something.

The creepers appeared to be a key part of the aliens' strategy. They needed to complete this mission, get one of the ugly animals back to the Enclave, and let all the super-smart people back there find a way to neutralize the monsters.

The Hawk swept in lower, remaining a safe distance away from the power station and Gizzida encampment. Finally, Finn pulled the quadcopter into a hover.

They were going to rappel down. The four of them rose, pulled their packs on, and clipped onto the rappelling lines.

"Good luck," Finn called back from the cockpit. "Call me for a pickup."

Shaw slammed the door back, his long-range laser rifle over one shoulder and the tranquilizer rifle over the other.

Claudia went first, diving out of the Hawk in a practiced move. Cam followed, simply stepping out of the quadcopter. The wind rushed into her face as she dropped downward.

As soon as her boots hit the ground, she disconnected from the line at a run, and headed toward the nearby trees.

The men followed, and the four of them moved in tight formation. They ran up the hill, dodging around the trees and making straight for the summit.

Finally, Claudia gave a hand signal, and they stopped.

"Over there," the woman murmured, motioning to a clear space that gave them a perfect view of the hive of activity down in the valley below.

They moved into position, and Cam lay down on her belly, pulling her binocs off her belt. Around her, the others were doing the same.

She slowly turned knobs on her binocs, and the view came into focus. What had looked like ants scurrying around on the ground were aliens, and there were a lot of them. *Damn*. There were a large number of raptor soldiers, as well as canids and hellion hunting dogs, and lots and lots of creepers.

"We need to lure a creeper away from the crowd," Claudia said. "If we can get it out of view of the main pack, then we can take it down without drawing too much attention."

Cam assessed the situation, studying the locations of the creepers, and then looking down the base of the hill where they were situated. "The hill curves around down there." She pointed. "If we lured one of the creepers around the base, it would put them out of view. Then we should have no trouble taking it down with the sedatives."

"What's this 'we' business?" Shaw grumbled.

Cam rolled her eyes. "Don't worry, no one will claim your shot, super sniper."

"Look." Claudia pointed. "There's a small group of creepers moving closer to us. Six creatures."

The others followed her gesture. Cam saw the group, along with a lone raptor soldier. They had broken away from the main camp. From a distance, the raptor looked almost human, but through the binocs, his scale-covered features and teeth-filled mouth reminded her that he wasn't.

"It almost looks like he's—"

"Their shepherd," Hemi finished. "Their keeper."

She nodded. "Whatever he's doing, we don't want his attention." She studied the group of creepers. They seemed placid enough, as though they were relaxed and not expecting any trouble.

"What are we going to lure it with?" Claudia asked.

Hemi grinned. "Me."

His words were like a kick to Cam's gut. God, she hadn't even thought that far ahead. She knew Hemi was scary-courageous to the point of being fearless.

She cleared her throat. "Let's talk through all the options—"

All of a sudden, the bushes nearby rustled. The four of them leaped to their feet, swinging their carbines up.

The thick bushes were shaking. Something was in there.

God, did the aliens know they were there? Tense, they all watched and waited. Cam's nerves stretched tighter and tighter.

Hemi made a small, frustrated sound, then stomped over to the bush.

"Hemi!" Cam snapped.

He ignored her and reached the bushes, peering over the top of them. "Shit." He swung his carbine over his shoulder, and then dived into the greenery.

"Fucking hell," Shaw breathed. "Goddamn crazy berserkers."

Cam rushed forward, the two Hell Squad soldiers flanking her. The bushes were shaking like crazy now, and she heard Hemi grunt. He was wrestling with something.

"Hemi," Cam said again. She kept her eye to her scope, ready to take a shot.

Suddenly, he reared up. Cam's throat went tight. Her gaze zeroed in on the giant alien spider in his arms, struggling to clamp onto his face. It was about the size of a basketball.

Damn. They'd been attacked by a swarm of these once, on their mad rush out of Blue Mountain Base. She scanned their surroundings, searching for more. They were *not* nice creatures.

She moved closer. "Dammit, Hemi. Throw it down and give us a clear shot."

Hemi spun, muscles straining, as he kept the creature from sucking onto his face. "Can't shoot it...might alert that raptor."

Shit, he was right. The last thing they needed was to let the Gizzida know they were here.

Hemi spun again, still wrestling with the creature, and he let out a huge laugh.

Crazy man. He was *enjoying* himself. Then his hands shifted, and she heard the crack of breaking bone.

He tossed the broken creature down, his chest heaving like bellows. He stood there, blood on his gloved hands, grinning.

Cam felt her pulse racing like an out-of-control Hawk. The moron. The fearless, macho moron.

***

Hemi grabbed one of their water bottles, and washed off the alien blood. He heard Shaw and Claudia hammering out the details for luring a creeper closer. Cam was unusually quiet. He glanced her way and saw her face was set like stone.

"Right," Shaw said. "I'll get into position." The sniper was loading the sedatives into the tranquilizer rifle. "Hemi, you need to bring the creeper in close enough for me to take a shot."

"Got it," Hemi replied.

Shaw looked at the women. "Claudia and Cam, you'll be his backup. If he gets into any trouble…"

"You mean, like getting up close and personal with an alien and getting himself eaten?" Cam asked.

Her sharp tone made Shaw shoot Hemi a sympathetic look.

Oh yeah, Cam was pissed.

"If he gets into any trouble, you two have the nets and stun prods. Carbines are for worst-case scenario. If you need to lay down cover fire, that'll let the aliens know we're here."

Hemi knew if they had to fire their carbines, then they'd be pointing a huge neon sign at themselves, and screw the mission. Aliens would descend on them in minutes.

"I'll get the damn thing here," Hemi said.

Suddenly, Cam stormed up to him and slammed her gloved fist into his gut. He grunted. With his armor on, it didn't hurt him, but she still packed a wallop.

"Are you trying to get yourself killed?" she snapped.

Yep, really mad. "No."

"You jumped into those bushes with no thought, no plan, no—"

He grabbed her shoulders. "I knew if we shot the damn thing, the aliens would've heard. I wanted to protect the mission." And you.

He kept his mouth shut on the second part. He was well aware that Cam could take care of herself. If she knew he was trying to protect her, mad would be the least of his worries. But it wouldn't stop him from doing what he could to keep her safe. He figured it was best not to tell her, though.

"And now you're going to make yourself bait for a damn creeper." Anger vibrated in her voice.

He reached out and cupped her cheek. "Cam, I'll be fine."

"You think I care if you get eaten by an alien?"

She lifted her chin at a haughty angle.

Yeah, he did. He could see the worry in her brown eyes, even if she couldn't admit it. "The plan will work."

"And if it doesn't?" she countered.

"I have a Plan B."

She frowned. "And what's Plan B?"

He winced. "Let's just hope Plan A works out."

Cam squeezed her eyes shut for a few seconds, then released a long breath. The next thing he knew, she grabbed the front of his armor and yanked him close.

"Don't get yourself killed, Rahia."

"Dying isn't part of the plan."

She lowered her voice so only he could hear. "If you do, you won't get to claim your prize."

Shit. An image of her lips stretched around— He mentally cursed, his cock twitching. He grinned at her. "Roger that."

They all headed down the hill, and Hemi forced himself to focus on his part of the mission. At the base of the hill, they stayed in cover under the trees. Shaw gave Claudia a quick kiss and nodded at Hemi and Cam. Then he disappeared into the trees.

He would circle around the hill to the location they'd selected. He'd get ready and wait for Hemi to lure the creeper around to him, well out of view of any other aliens.

Hemi pulled his carbine off and handed it to Cam. He checked his combat knife and his backup knife. He nodded at the women, then looked out into the valley.

He saw a group of creepers ahead. They were skittering around, two scuffling with each other. Their glowing orange bellies were empty. One raised its head and screeched.

Damn, they were ugly motherfuckers.

He glanced at his watch, pushing the protective cover off the face. Shaw should have had enough time to get into position.

A creeper wandered closer to them, and he felt Cam and Claudia tense. *Come on, creeper. Just a little closer.*

Just a few more meters, and it would be a good distance from the group and out of the direct line of sight of the raptor soldier babysitting them.

Closer. Closer. It was close enough now for Hemi to see the hard, black outer shell. It looked more like an insect than the raptors. He saw its sucker mouth moving.

It was now or never.

Hemi stepped out of the trees. At first, the alien didn't notice him. He watched it lower its head to the grass.

What was it doing? Its movements increased, and that's when he realized. It was sniffing the ground.

The creature lifted its head and looked his way. He saw glowing, red eyes lock onto him. Hemi started walking backward. He needed to get around the hill, well away from the other creepers, and close to Shaw. He had about a hundred meters to reach the sniper.

Walk in the park. Hemi kept moving steadily, not taking his gaze off the animal. The creeper was following him.

Suddenly, it stopped.

"Come on, you ugly motherfucker," he muttered. He kept his tone calm and coaxing.

Suddenly, the creeper bolted toward him with a blast of speed.

Shit. Hemi turned and ran.

He leaped over a fallen tree, and skirted around the hill. He heard the alien running close behind him. He smelled the stench of it.

Ahead, he spotted the trees Shaw had selected as his position. Just another twenty meters.

Something slammed into Hemi's legs and he went down, rolling across the grass.

He rolled onto his back and saw the creeper looming over him. It'd knocked his legs out from under him.

He yanked out his combat knife. The creature jabbed at him with one of its sharp legs.

"Hemi! Move!" Cam's frantic voice in his earpiece.

"You're still out of range," Shaw said. "Get it closer!"

Hemi rolled right beneath the creeper, dodging all six legs. The confused creeper turned in a circle, searching for him. Hemi pushed to his feet, dodged between the legs, and started sprinting.

"Come on, Hemi," Cam said. "Just a bit farther."

He felt something slam into his back, a sharp tip piercing his armor between the center of his shoulder blades. It sent him stumbling.

He recovered and kept charging. *Just pretend you're on the rugby field, Rahia.*

Ahead, he saw Cam and Claudia break out of the trees. Both of them were holding containment nets.

Cam tossed hers, and it flew through the air. The creeper screeched and dodged. The net skimmed over the creature but missed.

The creeper spun, and its gaze locked on Cam. She was out in the open now, a clear target.

It charged toward her.

"No, you don't," Hemi growled.

He leaped at it, stabbing his knife at its orange belly. It turned, rearing and lifting its two front legs off the ground. They waved madly.

Good. Now its attention was back on him.

"Still out of range," Shaw yelled.

Hemi saw the creeper tense. Then before he could move, the big, ugly sucker mouth pointed right at him.

Fuck. He turned, pumping his arms as he tried to run.

The mouth slammed down on him and closed around him. The world went black.

Chapter Seven

Hemi had just been swallowed by a creeper.

Cam fought back the panic threatening to choke her. She'd done it a hundred times before on previous missions, but what she felt now was overwhelming.

She ran at the creeper. Hemi only had seconds, minutes, who the hell knew? There was no room for out-of-control emotions in a life-or-death situation.

"Fuck me." Shaw's horrified voice echoed over the comm line.

Cam swung her carbine off her shoulder. Nearby alien raptor be damned. "Concentrate fire on its head." They couldn't risk hitting Hemi.

She didn't care if the noise brought every alien on the goddamn planet down on their heads. She was getting him out of there.

As Cam opened fire, Claudia's carbine fire joined hers. A bad taste filled Cam's mouth. Could he breathe in there? Was the transformation process starting already?

She saw several precise shots hit the creeper's eye, making it rear up. *Yes, Shaw.*

Together, the three of them advanced on the creeper. Its belly was swollen and bulging. *God.* Its legs slammed down again, and it spun in an unsteady circle.

The creature screamed under the hail of laser fire, and started shaking. Then it reared up again, legs waving madly.

Suddenly, Cam saw its belly split open in a long vertical gash. There was a rush of orange fluid, and then a large object fell out.

Hemi rose up on his knees with a roar, holding his combat knife in one hand.

Behind him, the creeper teetered like it was drunk, then its legs went out from under it and it collapsed.

"Woo hoo! That was one ride I don't want to do again," Hemi called out.

He looked like something out of a horror movie. He was coated in orange goo, his hair plastered to his head.

"Jesus." Cam ran to him, her heart thumping like a drum in her chest, and leaned down. "Are you okay?"

"Hell, yeah." Then he leaned over, falling on all fours, and vomited.

She crouched beside him, gingerly touching his back. She didn't give a damn that he was covered in alien goop. He was alive. "Get it all out, big guy."

He managed a nod. When he sank back on his hunches, his face was a little pale but he was smiling.

"You are one tough guy, Hemi," Claudia said.

Alive. Grinning, like he'd just done something fun.

One part of Cam just wanted to reach out and wrap herself around him, and hold on tight. It was a part of her that terrified her. She reached for her anger instead. "What the hell were you doing?"

He lifted his head. "Cam, baby—"

"Don't baby me," she yelled. "You let yourself get swallowed by an alien."

"I'm okay."

"You were gone. Inside an *alien*." Cam realized she was panting. A solid ball of emotion was lodged in her throat.

Hemi pushed to his feet and reached for her. "Cam."

She managed to pull herself together and took a step back. "You touch me with that gunk all over you, and I'll shoot you."

He grinned at her, his standard shit-eating grin, and seeing it settled her a little. He was alive, and he was okay.

"Ah, guys?" Shaw said. "We have company."

They all spun, carbines swinging around.

Nearby, another creeper was watching them, and standing beside it was the raptor keeper.

The raptor pivoted and started to run. Cam's jaw locked. No doubt to raise the alarm.

"I'll get the raptor," Claudia shouted, as she took off in pursuit. "You guys get the creeper."

The creeper screeched. It wasn't running.

It was staring at Hemi, Cam, and Shaw.

Then, it rushed forward in a dizzying burst of speed.

***

Hemi swiped gunk off his face, his gaze zeroing in on the creeper. This bad boy was going down.

"Come on," he shouted. "Shaw, get out of the way and get that fucking sedative ready."

The sniper backed up. "Give me a minute."

"You're crazy." Cam stepped up beside Hemi. "You just got eaten, and all of the aliens will know we're here, any minute now. We need to go."

Hemi snatched the stun prod off his belt. With a shake, it extended. The creeper came closer and closer. "Planning to get myself a little revenge first."

Beside him, he saw Cam grab her stun prod, as well.

The creature skittered forward, and Hemi lunged at it, leading with the stun prod. The weapon touched scaly skin and he heard a sizzle.

The creeper paused, but didn't seem worried, and it certainly wasn't stunned.

Damn. "Need to find its sensitive spots," he said. "Any place where the skin's not so tough."

He and Cam circled the creature. It watched them with burning red eyes. Hemi scanned the thick, black shell, searching for anywhere that might be more vulnerable.

It spun to watch them, raising its front legs. Cam leaped forward, and shoved her stunner against its chest.

This time, it jerked back and made a screeching sound. Still not stunned.

"The belly is softer," Hemi said.

"But you have to get past those legs, and put yourself at risk of getting eaten." Her gaze was hard as granite. "You are *not* doing that again."

He frowned, studying the now-wary creature again. He spied something.

"On its back," he said. "There's a soft spot right on the back of its head." It was a paler patch of skin.

Cam craned her neck. "I see it."

He gripped the back of her armor. "I'll throw you up there. You stun it."

She kept her body relaxed, and nodded. He gripped her waist and, using his own strength, combined with his exoskeleton, he tossed her up in the air.

Cam landed gracefully on the alien's back. Instantly, she went to her knees, grabbing onto the scaly hide.

It started bucking like a rodeo bull. As it spun, trying to knock her off, Hemi jumped in front of it. He needed to distract the damn thing and keep its attention on him.

He saw Cam scrambling to get closer to the weak spot, the stun prod clutched in her hand. But with the creeper shaking like a wild bronco, she couldn't take the shot.

All of a sudden, she flew off. She hit the ground and rolled. Hemi raced over to her, yanking her to her feet.

"Damn, it's a stubborn bastard," he muttered.

"Like someone else I know."

Hemi smiled. "You love it."

She snorted. "New plan. Disable it. Aim for the legs."

They went in together this time, both of them swinging their stun prods. The creeper swiped at them with its sharp legs. Hemi dodged and saw Cam rolling out of the way.

As they continued to antagonize the creeper, slamming the prods into the creature's legs, Hemi realized how much he liked working side by side with Cam. She was strong, smart, and gutsy.

He swung his prod again and this time heard a crunch.

The creeper let out an ear-splitting screech. It held up its broken leg, moving backward. But then it stared at them and charged.

Uh oh. It was really angry now.

Hemi lunged sideways, knocking Cam out of the way. He heard her swear and one of the creeper's legs slammed into his gut with the force of a baseball bat. The air rushed out of him and he went down on one knee.

When he looked up, he saw that sucker mouth rushing down at him.

Not again.

"You are *not* eating him again." Cam leaped over Hemi, planting her boot in his back and using him as a launch pad. She jumped up and jammed the stun prod into the alien's ugly, gaping mouth.

The creature shuddered. On the soft flesh of the mouth, the prod worked.

Thwap. Thwap.

Hemi registered the sound and saw two darts sticking into the alien's belly. It staggered back, took two ungainly steps to the side and collapsed.

Shaw jogged over to them. "Everyone okay?"

Cam blew out a breath. "Yes."

"Hell yeah." Adrenaline was punching through Hemi's system. He spun, swept an arm around Cam and yanked her to him. He crashed his mouth down on hers.

She wrestled for a couple of seconds. He knew he was covering her in alien goo, but dammit, he felt gloriously alive.

Then she kissed him back and he forgot about everything else.

"You two done?" Claudia's dry, amused voice.

Hemi reluctantly raised his head. He saw Shaw grinning at them, and Claudia walking closer. The woman was dragging a dead raptor behind her.

"I wish I didn't have to be," Hemi said. "But, yes."

Claudia dumped the raptor body.

"Hey, sweetie," Shaw said. "How'd it go?"

Claudia shot him a look. "Good. Killed the raptor. You?"

"Tranquilized the creeper before it ate Hemi or Cam."

Hemi snorted. "Right. And Cam and I just sat back and had a beer."

Claudia crouched and patted the raptor down. She pulled something off the leather straps that crisscrossed the alien's scaly chest. She held it up.

Hemi instantly recognized the black object. One

of the alien's data storage cubes.

"Geek squad should be able to get something off it." Claudia slipped the cube into her backpack. "Now, we need to get sleeping beauty out of here before reinforcements arrive."

Hemi pulled a device off his belt. It was a small silver box. He pressed the button on the side and it opened up into a stretcher. The iono-stretcher hovered off the ground.

"Need a hand," he said.

Shaw stepped up on the other side of the creature, with some grunting and a few curses, they wrestled the creeper onto the stretcher.

Claudia looked at her watch. "We have a lot of ground to cover before we get far enough away for a Hawk to land and load the creeper."

Hemi glanced toward the west. The sun would set in a few hours. *Shit.* They had a tight window if they were going to manage a pickup before nightfall.

"I'll hide the raptor body and then let's get moving," Claudia said. "We'll contact the Enclave and then work out our next movements."

"And let's find a river to dunk Hemi in." Cam's nose wrinkled. "You stink."

He bumped a shoulder against her, laughing when she tried to dodge away. "You'll have to join me. You're covered in as much muck as I am. I'm happy to wash your back."

"In your dreams, Rahia."

Oh, yeah. Hemi nudged the stretcher to get it moving as Claudia dragged the raptor body toward the trees. He was planning to have sweet, sweet dreams.

Chapter Eight

After an hour of hiking through the Snowy Mountains, they were back in drone range.

Cam leaned against a tree, watching as Claudia touched her earpiece, talking to her comms officer, Elle. Behind Claudia, Shaw and Hemi were keeping an eye on the sedated creeper. The men still didn't trust that the thing was knocked out.

She glanced west, at the burn of orange lining the sky. Night was falling.

Finally, Claudia lowered her arm and turned to look at them. "The Enclave confirmed that it's too late for them to come and pick us up. We'll need to hole up for the night."

Cam glanced at the creeper. "Do we have enough sedatives to keep that thing asleep all night?"

"Let's hope so," Claudia answered. "Emerson said we should be fine, and to give the creeper a top-up every few hours."

"So, what now?" Hemi asked.

"Elle says there is a camping area with a lodge in the National Park, not too far from here."

"Well, it is a lovely day for a stroll," Shaw said cheerily.

Hemi and Shaw pushed the iono-stretcher,

maneuvering the creeper around the trees. They trekked deeper into the forest, the shadows deepening as the day gave way to night.

Cam glanced at Hemi. The alien fluid had long ago dried, and formed an orange crust on his armor. There was still some streaking his dark hair, but other than that, he looked recovered from nearly being an alien meal.

She worked up a light sweat as they hiked through the hills, but Cam couldn't complain about the extended exercise, since it was nice to be outside in the fresh air. Even if they had to drag a freaky alien along with them.

"We should almost be there," Claudia said.

Moments later, the trees cleared, and they stood at the start of a narrow valley.

"Nice," Shaw drawled.

"Welcome to the Yarrangobilly Caves House," Claudia said.

A low building sat up on the side of the hill. It was an old, heritage-style house, made of cream wood, with a burgundy roof. A set of steps had been carved into the hill, leading up to it.

Down in the bottom of the valley was...a swimming pool?

"Elle says there are some amazing caves near here," Claudia said. "They used to be a big tourist attraction. And the pool is a thermal pool, fed by a natural spring."

"Looks like it has one of those fancy, high-tech, self-cleaning systems, too," Shaw said gleefully. "Not a leaf in sight."

Cam squinted, and then she noticed steam rising off the water. "Damn, I forgot my bikini."

Hemi turned, spearing her with a hot look. Shaw winked.

The four of them trekked up the steps to the house. It had a wide verandah covered in dust and leaves.

"What will we do with the creeper?" Hemi asked.

Claudia's brow creased. "Keep it out here on the verandah. Whoever is on watch can keep an eye on it, and give it the required shots of sedative."

The men secured the alien on the verandah. The door wasn't locked, and inside was almost as dusty as outside. The simple, old-world furniture was in keeping with the style of the house.

After striding through the house, and examining all the guestrooms, Cam claimed one, setting her carbine on the bed. Hemi took the room next to hers, and Claudia and Shaw took the room at the end of the hall.

Cam left her lower armor on, just in case, but stripped off her upper armor. When she met the others in the hall, she saw they'd done the same thing.

Darkness had now fallen, and Shaw clicked on a flashlight. "Let's eat. We'll have ourselves a nice little dinner party of rations."

Outside, they found a paved patio area, with overturned wooden furniture. They righted some of the chairs, and Shaw left the light on the table. Soon, they had all settled in, munching on their makeshift meals.

Cam tipped her head back, staring up at the stars peppering the night sky.

"My mum took me camping once," Claudia murmured. "It was terrible. Two city girls out in the bush. I didn't sleep a wink, I got attacked by mosquitoes, and it was hot as hell."

Shaw stared out into the darkness. "No camping in our house." His tone was dark. "My father was never sober enough."

Cam sensed a story there, but her thoughts turned to her own family. They'd camped in the Scottish Highlands a few times in the summer. She remembered that her parents had fought the entire time, and she'd been miserable. "We did a bit of camping." She left it at that.

Hemi stretched back on a lounger, lying with one arm tucked under his head. "We camped all the time." He smiled. "My parents owned land out of town, and with my brothers and my cousins always at our place, we were always setting up tents or camping under the stars. Mostly, we just wanted to start fires. My Ma would make us way too much food and we'd all stay up way too late. Pretty sure my stepdad snuck up to check on us in the night."

There was so much affection in his voice. Cam hunched forward, her emotions a tight ball in her belly. His life was nothing like her family experience, at all.

The conversation shifted, and she listened to Hemi's deep voice as he talked with Shaw and Claudia. But in her head, images were flicking through like they were on fast-forward.

Of Hemi getting sucked inside that damn creeper. Of how she'd felt, realizing he was inside the alien and could die.

She needed some breathing room. "Who's got first watch?" she asked.

"Me," Shaw answered. "Then Claudia, Hemi, and then you."

"Good." Cam shot to her feet. Her emotions were boiling, and she needed to get them under control. "I'm going for a swim."

***

Hemi held a flashlight, and followed the steps down to the pool.

He heard the sound of a body moving through the water. He wasn't sure what had upset Cam, but he'd watched her enough to know all her moods, and she'd been sad when she'd left.

He approached the pool, and saw Cam's armor stacked by the pool edge. She was moving with long, even strokes. He knew she loved to swim. Whenever she got the chance, she was in the indoor pool at the Enclave. And he loved to watch her, and not only because of the way she rocked a bikini.

Standing at the edge, he watched her tumble, push off, and head back the length of the large thermal pool. He realized there was something soothing about watching her.

Finally, she noticed him and stopped, treading water in the center of the pool. They stared at each other.

"Don't you have an alien to wrestle?" she said. "A risk to take?"

So, whatever was bothering her was now aimed his way. He felt a flicker of heat and started pulling off his armor. "I'm sorry I scared you."

"I wasn't scared," she said quickly. "I always thought you wild berserkers were courageous and fearless, but I think you're just reckless."

She kicked over to the side and pushed out of the water. He'd wondered if she was naked, but she was wearing her underwear—a black sports bra and boy-style panties. Water streamed off her.

"You were scared," he repeated. "But I'm okay." He held his arms out.

She made a scoffing sound. "Don't flatter yourself, Rahia—"

He grabbed her shoulders, pulling her close.

She tried to pull away from him. "The pool's all yours."

He reeled her in closer. "Cam."

She made a short sound and then went up on her toes. Before he knew it, her mouth was on his— hard and angry.

He groaned, yanking her up, and letting his tongue plunder her mouth.

The kiss deepened, and Hemi shuddered. He fisted a hand in her hair, tilting her head back to give him better access to that mouth of hers.

She moaned. "Do not get eaten again."

He heard the emotion in her voice and it made his gut tight. "I won't." He boosted her up, lifting her so she wrapped her legs around his waist.

She ground against him. "I hurt," she murmured. "I hurt all over for you, Hemi."

Fuck. The raw honesty in her voice slammed into him. "I need to be inside you, Cam. I need it hard. Brutal."

She reached up, biting the side of his neck. "Yes."

Hemi stepped off the edge and dropped into the water. The warmth surrounded them, and he kissed her beneath the water. It was like a private cocoon that enveloped them.

Then they popped up above the surface, the cooler night air a contrast to the warm water. Not to mention the heat of the woman in his arms. He nipped her lips, skating his tongue over them, before he pushed her lips apart. He worked his tongue inside her mouth, loving her needy moans. He wanted to claim her, make sure she knew exactly who she belonged to.

She rubbed against him, a lithe move of her hips. She knew she was rubbing that sexy warmth of hers against his hard cock. His palms flexed on her ass.

"Damn." He nipped her bottom lip. "You're begging to be fucked, aren't you, baby?"

She undulated against him again. "Hemi, less talk, more action."

He slid a hand down her toned belly and inside her panties. "I'll make it stop hurting."

He was about to caress her, when he heard a splash in the water behind her.

Hemi felt her stiffen in his arms. He looked over

her shoulder and she swiveled her head to do the same. From the faint glow of his flashlight on the edge, he saw a ripple across the otherwise smooth surface.

"What the hell was that?" Cam unwrapped her legs from around him.

He set her down and they moved apart, both of them searching the water. Hemi reached out on the edge and grabbed his knife from his gear.

"Get out," he ordered.

She ignored him. "Maybe it was some native animal."

"Maybe."

A shadow moved at the end of the pool.

Cam relaxed. "Look."

He saw the lizard climb out of the pool and dart away. Damn thing could have been Gizzida, if it was bigger. The good-size lizard had a ridge of spikes on its back. "A water dragon."

But before he could say anything else, they heard another splash. Closer this time.

He and Cam traded a glance. Hemi's nerves pulled tight. Something else was in the water with them, and it wasn't a friendly lizard. Hell, the water dragon had probably been fleeing.

Suddenly, Cam cursed.

"Cam?"

She kicked her leg, splashing the water. Her gaze met his, her eyes wide. His gut went hard as a rock and he took one step toward her.

Then she was yanked under the water.

No!

Chapter Nine

Sharp claws dug into her leg.

Cam kicked hard against her attacker. Bubbles churned the water, and her lungs were starting to burn.

Air. She needed air.

With another savage kick, she managed to dislodge her attacker. She shot to the surface and the cooler night air hit her face. She dragged in a quick breath, but a second later, she felt those sharp claws again, and she was pulled back under.

She struggled, bubbles rushing past her face. She kicked and punched at the creature.

Suddenly, she felt a hand at the back of her neck. She was yanked up, and came face-to-face with an enraged Hemi.

He gave a vicious stab of his combat knife and she heard an animal hiss. Those razor-sharp claws released. Hemi pushed her aside and dived into the water.

Cam blinked, her chest heaving, trying to get her brain to start firing.

Hemi rose out of the water, yanking something out with him.

He wrestled with the creature, splashing in the

water. It wasn't large—about the size of a big house cat—but it was mad. She had no idea what it had originally been—dog, cat, possum, who the hell knew? But now the damn thing was scaly, and had sharp, slashing claws.

Cam dragged in more air, and waded closer to the fight. The demonic creature was making hissing noises, and Hemi was trying to hold it still enough to attack it with his knife.

She grabbed the hilt of the knife. "You hold the damn thing."

He released the knife with a nod. He clamped both hands on the creature and in the light from the flashlight, she saw his muscles bulging.

Cam lifted the blade, waiting. As the man and animal struggled, she caught a good look at the creature.

It had once been a water dragon. A beautiful, graceful lizard turned into an abomination.

She stabbed at it, again and again. It slashed out, opening deep scratches in Hemi's forearm. She stabbed it again, single-mindedly. Blood splattered into the water around them. With a harsh noise, the mutated animal curled in on itself and flopped in Hemi's hands.

With a curse, he spun and tossed it out of the pool.

Jesus. Cam collapsed against the side of the pool.

"You hurt?" Hemi's deep voice shattered the quiet.

She bit her lip. Her calf was burning. "My leg—"

With three large steps, he charged through the water and scooped her into his arms. Cam thought about complaining about him carting her around like some damsel, but the truth was, she liked it when Hemi carried her. She was a tall, muscular woman, and there'd never been too many men who could do that.

He climbed the steps out of the pool, and then set her down carefully on the grass by the flashlight. For a big, tough guy, he could be gentle when he chose to be.

As he crouched, he probed her leg, his eyebrows drawn together in a frown. She just stared at him. He was wet, his hair slicked back, and his dark beard glistened, too. He hadn't hesitated to jump in to help her.

So Hemi. She'd accused him of being reckless, but maybe he just couldn't help himself. If someone needed help, he was going to help. He was a hero—with tattoos and rough edges.

"Scratched you up pretty bad," he rumbled.

Running footsteps came up behind them.

"You guys okay?"

Cam looked over her shoulder, and saw Claudia and Shaw coming toward them. Shaw was carrying a first aid kit.

"We're fine. Some mutated alien creature decided to take a swim and a bite out of Cam," Hemi told them.

Shaw set the kit down. "Ouch."

Hemi opened the pack, and set to work cleaning her scratches.

"You two think you can avoid trouble for the rest of the night?" Claudia asked dryly.

"I'll try." Hemi winked. "But no promises."

"Berserkers," Claudia muttered. The Hell Squad soldiers headed back up to the house.

As Hemi tended her wound, Cam's pulse jumped erratically. She watched his expression—all careful concentration—and the gentle way he touched her skin. Dammit, it was hard to resist him when he was sweet.

So many emotions were churning up together inside her. But it was fear that was making her mouth go dry.

"You going to tell me why you got uncomfortable talking about camping and family back at dinner?"

She blinked, trying to follow the sudden turn in the conversation. He wanted to talk about this now? "No."

"Cam." A firm tone.

She huffed out a breath. "I didn't have brothers, sisters, and a gaggle of cousins." She winced. Even she heard the defensive tone of her voice. "My camping trips were stiff and soulless, except for when my parents fought."

"Your parents didn't get along?"

"That's an understatement. They'd loved each other once. Passionately, by all accounts." It was why she didn't trust intense, out-of-control emotions. "My mother told me all about the handsome doctor working in Kenya who'd swept the beautiful aid worker off her feet. They had a whirlwind, passionate romance, and were married

93

a few months later."

"Your mother left Kenya."

Cam nodded. "Yes, she moved to Scotland with her handsome doctor." She'd left her friends, her family, her work, everything she'd known…

"And?"

"I'm sure you can guess the rest." The romance had turned sour. Passion had turned to poison. Love had turned to something ugly. "Love is a double-edged sword."

Hemi pressed a bandage over the wounds. "There. You get the doc to check it out properly when we get back to base."

Their eyes met, and she nodded.

Suddenly, he leaned forward. His lips met hers, and this time the kiss was slow and deep.

His fingers feathered through her hair. For once, desire wasn't a wild explosion, but a slower, inexorable build up.

His lips moved to her jaw, his beard scraping her skin.

When he pulled back, the flashlight cast shadows over part of his face. "I don't know what went wrong for your parents, Cam, but family isn't like that for everyone."

Cam fought the urge to hunch her shoulders. He saw too much. He made her want too much. Dangerous things that she knew better than to want.

"Look Hemi, you want to fuck, we'll fuck. That's it. No talking about family or what's upsetting us."

His hand moved, stroking along her jaw. "We're

more than that, and you know it."

His hand slid down, along her neck, and cupped her breast. He flicked a thumb across her nipple. Goose bumps broke out on her skin, and she swallowed a moan.

This. This she could deal with. As desire flared, warming her up, she focused solely on that. "I'm burning up."

"When you admit that this is more, I'll make the burning stop."

She narrowed her eyes at him. "You're giving me an ultimatum?"

"I'm trying to get through those damn barriers you build," he muttered.

"You're using sex as part of your ultimatum?"

He muttered a curse and she saw the frustrated edge of anger in his eyes. Then he pressed his mouth down on hers. Just as the kiss deepened, he pulled back.

"I want more than a fuck, Cam." He pushed to his feet. "I want all of you. So when you aren't too afraid to accept that, I'll be waiting."

***

He was an idiot.

Hemi stood in the early-morning light, watching as Hell Squad hooked up the creeper to the hovering Hawk, with heavy-duty cargo chains.

It had been a restless, but uneventful night. There'd been no more alien attacks, and the creeper had thankfully stayed sedated.

And Cam had ignored him.

Hemi had stayed semi-hard all night just thinking about those long legs of hers wrapped around his hips. He wanted her more than he damn well wanted to breathe, but he knew if he gave her what she thought she wanted, they'd stay locked in this damn loop of never getting closer. God, she was a pain in the ass.

She'd come around. He could wait her out.

His gaze found her, back in her armor, talking with Reed MacKinnon as they connected the line to the harness they'd wrapped around the creeper.

Hemi knew he just needed to stay strong. He wanted more than Cam's body. He wanted her to open up to him, so he could see more of both the passionate, laughing woman inside, and the hurt, jaded woman who was protecting herself.

"Okay, let's get out of here," Marcus called out in his gravelly voice.

They climbed aboard the quadcopter, and Hemi watched as Cam moved as far away from him as she could. He sank down beside Shaw and gripped his carbine.

As the Hawk took off, everyone was tense. They'd be flying with a creeper suspended below the quadcopter. They may as well hang a glowing, neon sign from the craft for every Gizzida to see.

Soon, they were airborne and heading north. Hemi scanned the soldiers around him. Every one of them was excruciatingly aware that the alien encampment was only kilometers away, and they were heading toward the ruins of Sydney—a major hub for the aliens.

A shimmer outside the side window caught his attention. He leaned forward, and spotted another one whiz past.

Cam's squad was escorting them in the Darkswifts.

Stony-faced Marcus and Cruz were seated closest to the cockpit. Gabe, with his usual silent "don't fuck with me" face stood with Reed by the side door. The big man was stroking his carbine.

Hemi leaned back, closed his eyes, and crossed his palms over his stomach.

"Are you really relaxed, or are you just faking it?"

He opened one eye and saw Claudia watching him. "You guys are on edge enough for all of us put together. No point in me adding to it." He lifted a shoulder. "Doesn't help anyone."

"That's pretty Zen, Rahia."

He closed his eyes again. "My ma taught us boys how to chill out. She had three big, wild testosterone-filled sons. She figured if she didn't teach us to control ourselves, we'd end up in jail, or dead."

"Sounds like a woman I would like."

Cam's quiet comment made him open his eyes again. She was watching him, an unreadable expression on her face. "You would." And she'd be in fits of delight at the woman Hemi wanted to claim as his own.

Marcus pressed a finger to his earpiece. "Elle, any aliens in range?" He tilted his head as he listened to his wife's answer. "Good. Let's hope it stays that way."

It wasn't until the Hawk began to descend into the hangar at the Enclave that he felt the men and women around him start to relax.

Finn kept the Hawk hovering just above the ground, as the crew below disconnected the creeper. When the skids of the Hawk finally touched down, Marcus pulled the side door open.

As he climbed out, Hemi spotted Laura's red hair. She was shouting orders at her team as they shifted the creeper onto a larger, modified, iono-stretcher. He hoped to hell the cell they'd been preparing was strong enough. He suspected that once the creeper woke up, it was going to be royally pissed.

General Holmes stepped forward. "Well done."

"Thanks." Claudia tossed her ponytail over her shoulder. "We had a good team. And we had a lovely little retreat in the mountains."

Shaw groaned. "I need a shower and my own bed." Then he slapped Hemi on the back. "Not quite as much as this man, though. Apparently, creepers don't think berserkers taste bad."

"Screw you, Shaw," Hemi said good-naturedly.

"No accounting for taste," Cam added.

Tane approached. "You okay?"

"Fine."

"Heard you got swallowed by an alien."

Hemi grimaced. "I don't recommend it."

Tane peered at Hemi with that eerie stare of his. "You're sure you're okay?"

He wasn't ready to talk about Cam, even with his brother. He nodded. When he turned his head, he saw Cam stalk away, heading for the exit. Disappointment skewered him.

Suddenly, a wild, enraged screech filled the hangar. Hemi tensed and spun...in time to see one of Laura's team members go flying, his stun prod skidding across the concrete.

Laura was shouting, and the creeper was beginning to tear free of its restraints. One of its legs was slicing dangerously through the air.

Shit. Hemi charged forward. Around him, Hell Squad leaped forward, swinging carbines off their shoulders.

"Try not to kill it!" Hemi called out. He didn't fancy another hunting trip.

"We need it alive," the general added.

Another strap broke, and the creeper was now half on, half off the stretcher. Its hot, red gaze on the fallen guard.

"Sedatives are losing their effect," Laura yelled. She was wielding a stun prod, and looked like she knew how to use it.

"Find some chains, or something strong enough to contain it," Hemi told her. "I'll bring it down."

A man screamed.

Hemi saw the young guard scooting backward on his butt. The creeper was moving toward him, dragging the stretcher with it.

Hemi broke into a run. He needed a prod. He opened his mouth to yell, when he saw Cam running in closer from the other side. She was holding the downed guard's prod. She tossed it, and it spun through the air.

He snatched it, swung it around, and then threw himself into the air. He raised the prod above his head.

The creeper spun to face him, and let out a screech. Its ugly mouth was open and pulsing.

Hemi jammed the prod down into it.

The creeper dropped, its body doing a jerky dance as the stun hit it. Hemi sailed over the alien and hit the ground with a roll.

He came to his feet to the sound of applause.

Laura's team all looked shocked but relieved. Shaw was applauding and gave a whistle. "That was a nine-point-five, Rahia. If you could have added a mid-air flip, it would have been a perfect ten."

"I'll give you a flip." He gave the sniper the finger.

Their banter broke the edgy tension in the room. There was a clank of chains.

"Get that damn thing chained up and in its cell," Laura ordered. "Thanks, Hemi. Cam."

He glanced at Cam and nodded. Without her help, they would have been cutting that poor guard out of the creeper. *Come on, Cam. Just reach out.*

She stared at him for a second, then walked out.

A muscle ticked in his jaw. He could wait her out, dammit. But his hands ached to touch her, grab her, and damn well shake some sense into her.

"Go, Hemi," the general said. "Clean up and get

some rest."

Back in his room, Hemi had a quick shower, and pulled on some jeans. In his small kitchen, he cracked open a beer, and leaned against the cupboards. He knew it wasn't even lunchtime yet, but he needed a drink.

After a mission he was always keyed up, energized. In the past, he'd sweet-talk a woman into his bed to work it off, or he'd hang with his squad.

All he wanted today, though, was Cam. Wrapped around him, him lodged inside her, her laugh ringing in his ears.

He took a long sip of beer. He was a man used to taking what he wanted, but with Cam, he knew he couldn't take her. Not when she'd chalk it up to desire, fucking, or a one-night stand. God, he felt like he was a crazy teenager again playing chicken in his car with his mates. Waiting to see which one would swerve first.

Screw this. He slammed his beer down. She didn't want to talk about her past or her family, fine. They'd get to that later. He'd fuck her hard and good, get her all soft and flushed, and then get his answers. He'd do whatever he had to do in order to get the rest of her.

He grabbed a shirt off the back of a chair and slipped it on, marching toward the door. She'd probably be in her room. Wherever she was, he'd find her. He yanked his door open.

Then he jerked to a stop. Cam was standing in his doorway, her fist raised to knock on his door.

"Oh, you're going out. Right." Her face fell and she started to turn away. "Whatever. I'll see you around—"

Hemi grabbed her arm to stop her. She'd come to him.

His gaze drifted over her. She'd showered as well, her hair still wet, and she was wearing teeny tiny denim shorts that showed every inch of those long, glossy legs of hers.

Lust hit him like a battering ram. He yanked her to him, and her hands went to his shoulders, digging in.

He wasn't sure if he kissed her or she kissed him, but their tongues tangled. He lifted her up, his palms digging into the globes of her ass, as she wrapped her legs around his waist.

He staggered inside, managing to close the door with a kick of his foot. He stumbled through his quarters, desperate for her. He hit something and heard a crash.

Flat surface. He needed the nearest hard, flat surface. He set her down, dimly realizing it was on his kitchen counter.

"Now. Now." She was chanting the words, her hands diving lower to drag down the zipper of his jeans. His cock sprang free and she circled it, stroked once.

A shudder wracked him. *Damn.* He reached up, gripping her short hair, and tipped her head back. Their mouths fused together.

The next thing he realized, her hands were tangled in his T-shirt, yanking it up. He pulled it off with one tug, and then yanked hers over her head.

"Mine," he growled. He pulled her up, sucking her nipple into his mouth.

"Hot. I'm so hot." She pressed her hands back onto the smooth counter and thrust her chest up. He'd never seen anything sexier.

He slid his other hand down, following the dip of her waist and the curve of her hips, until he reached her shorts. It took him seconds to strip them off her and get his hands between her legs.

"So wet. No wonder you're hurting, baby." He stroked her, feeling her hips move. "This is where I want to be. I belong here."

He pulled back, clamping his hands on her hips and dragging her to the edge of the counter.

"Hurry." She let her legs fall apart.

Hemi was moving on animal instinct now. Need was like the pound of his heartbeat in his head. He pulled her closer and thrust inside her. She cried out, her back arching.

God. He pressed his mouth to her neck, grazing her skin with his teeth.

Then he pulled back. "Watch. Look where we're joined." His voice was guttural.

He shifted so she could see where their bodies were connected. Where the thick part of him was splitting her wide.

She looked, her face flushed. She reached down, her hand stroking where she was strained around his cock. Then her long fingers moved up to brush her clit. She bucked.

"That's it, baby. Touch yourself." He started to pump into her.

As she caressed her clit and he moved inside her, his control eroded away. He was hammering into her now and he heard something fall off the counter and smash.

Her legs wrapped tight around him, her heels digging into his back. Guttural animal sounds emanated from both of them.

Then Cam arched and cried out. "Hemi! I'm coming."

He was completely lost in her and he fucking loved it. He felt her orgasm rocket through her, and her body clamped down on him, squeezing his cock. It tossed him over the edge. He kept his gaze locked on her face, not wanting to miss a single thing. He came with one long roar.

Chapter Ten

Hemi scooped Cam off the counter with one strong flex of his arm. Since her legs were boneless, she was okay with that. And because she was feeling pretty darn good, she let herself snuggle into his chest.

He laid her down on the bed. The sheets smelled of him—dark and masculine. Then he leaned over her and pressed a kiss to her shoulder.

The intimacy made her belly flutter.

His gaze raked over her. "So damn sexy, Cam." This time he pressed a kiss to her collarbone, his beard scraping her sensitive skin. She shivered.

"Hey, big guy." She tried to keep it easy, joking, and arched up into him. She scraped her nails down his bare chest, over bulky muscles and his tattoos. "You can't be ready for round two yet?"

He ignored her, and kept peppering soft kisses between her breasts, down her stomach. She started to squirm.

"I was coming to find you," he murmured.

She closed her eyes for a second. Hell, they were a pair.

"I'm still a bit pissed at you for the risks you took on the mission. And for getting eaten." She knew images of him disappearing inside that creeper would haunt her nightmares for a long while.

"And I still want you to tell me about your parents, and let me in." This time, he pressed a kiss to her belly, and then raised his head to look up her body. "But not now."

Her breath hitched, and she stared at the heat and intensity in his dark-brown eyes. "Not now."

But Cam already knew that the stubborn berserker would keep pushing and prodding her. She would share with him later, about the two people she'd come from, damn him. If for no other reason than to get him to see that she wasn't the forever kind of girl. That they wouldn't work, long term.

His mouth grazed over her hip bones, and his tongue scraped her skin. He nudged her legs apart.

His mouth went lower and her hands twisted in the sheets. She loved watching his big bulky body between her far more slender legs. Then his mouth was on her, sucking and licking, and her eyelids fluttered closed. His beard scraped against sensitive places.

"Look at me." A demanding growl.

Yeah, her Hemi liked to watch. His big palms slid under her butt and lifted her up to him. She watched his dark head between her legs as he sucked on her like she was his favorite fruit.

God. That tongue of his. With another lick, she came hard against his mouth.

When he set her back on the bed, Cam was

panting, fighting to come down from the high.

He rolled onto his back beside her, a very satisfied look on his face.

She got to her knees. "Pretty pleased with yourself, Rahia?"

His smile widened. He'd never be a handsome man, but that cocky grin of his made him damn delectable.

"Any time my woman screams my name in pleasure makes me pretty pleased."

His woman. Cam filed that away to deal with later. She let her fingers drift over his ridged stomach. "I seem to recall I owe you a prize."

His body went rigid. She pressed her hands to his strong thighs and scooted back a bit.

Then his hand feathered through her hair. "I won't lie. I've imagined my cock between your lips about a thousand times."

She circled the broad base of his cock and stroked. She loved going down on a man, having him at her mercy, seeing the raw pleasure on his face.

As she pumped his thick cock, he pulsed in her palm. God, he seemed even bigger than before. She lowered her head and sucked the thick head into her mouth.

Hemi groaned and muttered a curse.

Cam swirled her tongue around him, loving the salty, musky taste of him. She looked up his strong body, saw his glittering dark gaze locked on her. Like he'd never be able to look away.

"Tell me if there is anything you like." She

sucked him back in.

"My cock in your mouth. I'm happy." His next groan was deep and long. "You might destroy me, but I'll die a happy, satisfied man."

She took him deeper, experimenting with her grip and speed. Each groan told her what he liked best. Soon his hips were moving, and she knew he was getting closer to the edge.

His big hands were on the back of her head now, guiding her as she took him deeper.

"Baby. Fuck, I'm going to come."

She pulled back, licking at him. "You want to come in my mouth, or somewhere else?"

He muttered a vicious curse and yanked her up. She grinned, straddling his hips. She wasted no time circling his thick cock and sinking down on him.

They both groaned. Cam pressed her hands against his hard chest, and took a second to adjust. She felt every inch of him stretching her. She started to ride. She loved having a man beneath her, too. Correction—she loved having *this* man beneath her.

She shifted her hips, moving in circles for a bit, before she found her rhythm. She started riding him, faster and faster. His groans echoed around her, and the sensations built inside her.

"No." Hemi grabbed her hips and slowed her down. "I want slow and steady this time." His voice was deep, his eyes glittering. "I want to watch your lovely breasts jiggle when you move. I want to watch you take me slow and deep."

"I'm on top, Hemi. That means I'm in charge." And she wanted it hard and fast, not this slow, intimate ride that made her throat go tight.

But his hands dug into her hips, controlling her speed. The sensations kept growing, building, spilling around inside her.

"Hemi."

"That's it. I fucking love it when you say my name like that, when I'm deep inside you."

Her head fell back and she kept riding him.

"Eyes to me," he demanded.

She opened her eyes and met deep brown ones. Her hips kept rising and falling, and her orgasm curled around her, shining hot and bright.

Then she broke apart, sobbing as her climax hit her. Hemi groaned and bumped his hips up, prolonging the intensity of her pleasure. As his body bucked again under the force of his own release, Cam fell over the edge once more.

***

Cam felt far too good to let anything worry her. Her body was unbelievably loose, limber, and relaxed. She might have had beard burn in a few unmentionable places, but that didn't bother her, either. She'd been well compensated for it.

Hell, she even let Hemi hold her hand as they walked through the corridor on the way to the games room.

They were heading to meet his squad for a few drinks. She'd wanted to take off, but he'd grabbed her hand and refused to let go. And then he'd asked her nicely and had even said please.

His strong fingers squeezed hers. "It's just a beer, baby, relax."

Just a beer. Just enjoy yourself. But as she glanced down at their entwined fingers, she was more worried that there were other things entwined, as well. Things that she'd never get untangled.

Had her parents held hands? Looked at each other with such want and desire? She was sure they had...for a while.

A few people glanced at them as they passed. Their joined hands were met with a mixture of raised brows and smiles.

Cam ignored them, until they entered the games room. The place was definitely busy. Lots of people talking and laughing, finding their fun where they could. On the opposite side of the room, she spotted the men of Squad Three, throwing axes at a target.

Of course, they were throwing axes. She rolled her eyes, watching Tane slam a small axe into a bullseye on the wall. Why bother with darts or knives, when you could throw axes?

It looked like Tane and Levi were locked in a death match. Tane had his dark dreadlocks pulled back, and was sipping from a homebrewed beer, his face serious, as he pulled an axe from the target.

As Hemi and Cam approached, Tane's dark gaze fell on them. A faint smile crossed his face.

As the rest of Hemi's squad turned to look at them, Cam tried to pull her hand away from his.

Hemi held on tighter. They ended up in a tugging match.

Hemi won by yanking her in front of him, and wrapping an arm around her neck. It was a pretty blatant, macho-man claim. She barely stopped herself from rolling her eyes.

When she looked back at the men, she saw a close-to-full-blown smile on Tane's mouth. She went still and blinked. The man was seriously attractive under the scary intensity.

"You should smile more often," she said.

His smile widened a fraction.

Hemi's arm tightened, his beard tickling her ear. "Quit flirting with my brother."

"But I just realized how handsome he is, and—"

Hemi growled and nipped her ear, but she could tell he was grinning.

"Want a drink?" he asked.

"Sure."

As Hemi moved over to the self-service bar, Cam leaned against the wall.

"So you finally let Hemi catch you." The smooth voice belonged to Ash.

The tall, lean man would make any woman's mouth water. He was the handsome berserker, with a fallen-angel face and amazing colorful tattoos covering his arms. She saw something different in those designs every time she looked at them.

"He was starting to whine. It was kind of pathetic."

The berserkers broke into laughter. Cam noted a

woman nearby cast a wistful glance their way. Cam couldn't really blame the woman.

"My brother is a lucky man," a deep, booming voice said.

Cam glanced at the big man sitting nearby. "I think so."

Manu Rahia was a huge mountain of muscle. He looked like a mix of his brothers. Not quite as rugged as Hemi, and not quite as handsome as Tane. Sitting sprawled in a chair, you'd never guess one of his legs was a prosthetic. She remembered when he'd been injured on a mission. The berserkers had been dangerous to be around while they'd waited to hear if Manu would survive. Actually, Hemi had destroyed several chairs and put a few holes in the walls of Blue Mountain Base.

The oldest Rahia smiled, his teeth white against his bronze skin. "You'll keep him on his toes. Hemi needs that."

"Thank you...I think."

Manu's laugh was big and loud. It made her want to join in. He wasn't a man who let bitterness or regrets rule him.

"You come down to the firing range some time and I'll give you a few tips about Hemi."

She smiled. Having intel on Hemi could be useful, and she enjoyed spending time in the firing range. Manu ran a tight ship down there, and the man didn't let his prosthetic slow him down at all.

Hemi returned, clutching a bunch of beers. He handed out the beers before passing her one. Then, he leaned down and pressed a kiss to her shoulder.

"What lies is Manu telling you?"

A warm glow burst inside of Cam, and she struggled to ignore it. Hemi was affectionate, that was all. "He's tempting me with irresistible things."

Hemi's brows drew together. "Stay away from my woman."

Manu laughed again and Cam slapped at Hemi's shoulder. "He's offering me behind-the-scenes intel on keeping one step ahead of you."

Now Hemi grinned. "It won't help you."

Cam hitched herself up on a stool and sipped her beer. The axe-throwing contest was heating up and she turned to watch. Hemi stood close enough for her to feel the heat of him.

Levi lost by a whisker to Tane—amidst some ribbing—and Griff Callan stepped up next to challenge Tane. She didn't know Griff very well. He was a man who radiated a dangerous intensity. He was a hard-edged former cop who'd gone down for murder. She didn't know all his story, doubted anyone did, but for a cop to survive doing time in a Coalition Supermax prison... She shivered—he had to be hard. She'd heard he'd escaped during the invasion, somehow hooked up with the berserkers, and ended up at Blue Mountain Base.

Feminine giggles made her turn her head. A young, blonde woman was flirting with Levi. He was smiling at the woman, but Cam thought he looked distracted. He kept glancing across the room. She wondered what—or who—had caught his eye?

Cam's gaze fell on the final berserker. He was

sitting in a chair nearby, ice rattling in a glass of what looked like whiskey.

All the berserkers were in the running for being the most dangerous, badass guys in the Enclave. A few of the guys from Hell Squad could join them, too, and Roth was no slouch in the driven badass department. But when her eyes met Dom Santora's all she could think of was black ice. He had Italian good looks, swarthy skin, and a soulless gaze.

She leaned forward. "Were you really in the Mafia?"

From nearby, Levi turned and snorted. Dom just raised a dark brow. "Maybe."

Hemi's arm snaked over her shoulders. "He won't tell you. Dom is the king of being mysterious."

The man in question sipped his drink.

"Hemi, you're up." Tane handed an axe to his brother.

Hemi took it and headed over to join Griff. As the two men battled it out, Cam cheered Hemi on.

When he won, he raised a fist in the air. Griff groaned and went to grab a beer.

Hemi's gaze fell on Cam. "You up for a challenge, McNab?"

She pushed to her feet and sauntered over. She heard Levi whistle. She snatched up an axe, running her finger over the edge of it. She heard one of the berserkers laugh behind her.

"I can beat you with my eyes closed, Rahia."

"Uh oh." Ash shook his head and laughed.

Cam leaned over, conscious of Hemi's gaze

sliding to her ass. "I need a few practice throws first."

As she started throwing the axes, she realized it wasn't as easy as she'd thought. She adjusted and kept trying. A few throws went wide, earning her catcalls from the berserkers.

Hemi moved in behind her, his arms sliding around her. "Let me give you a few pointers." His warm breath on her neck made her shiver.

"I bet you say that to all the ladies."

He chuckled. "You need to get your grip on the axe right. Adjust to the weight of it. It's top-heavy, and not like throwing a knife."

With his help, her next few throws were better.

"Okay, Rahia. Let's play." She deliberately rubbed her ass against him.

His hands clamped on her hips. "You're trying to distract me."

She turned her head and fluttered her eyelashes. "I would never do that."

"Witch." He nipped her lips.

They settled on best of five, and she lost woefully. But hearing Hemi's deep laugh was worth it.

"You owe me another prize," he growled against her lips.

"And I always pay my debts." She happily bowed out and headed back to her stool. She watched Dom step up to take her place.

As the men gave each other a hard time, she sipped her beer and smiled. Tane, Manu, and Hemi might be the only ones related by blood, but she could see that these men were brothers.

She felt a presence at her side and glanced up. Tane loomed over her, his gaze on his brother.

"Thanks for rescuing him," Tane said quietly.

Something in her softened. "He cut his way out of that alien, Tane. Hemi rescued himself."

"You fought for him and made sure he came home."

Tane's face was expressionless, but she knew instantly that this man loved his brother. *Family*. It made her ache.

"Sure thing." She covered her reaction by taking another sip of her homebrew.

"And thanks for making him smile."

She raised a brow, surprised. "He's always smiling."

Tane's gaze met hers. "Not like he is now."

Tane moved away, and for a moment, Cam sat there, listening to the joking and ribbing between the berserkers. They were a wild bunch, but she knew they were a hell of a squad. Every one of them was willing to fight for those who needed their protection. Whatever they'd been before the invasion, they were heroes now.

Cam's gaze moved to Hemi, watching the flex of his muscles as he tossed an axe. She took a deep breath and let herself relax and just enjoy.

"The tech team is working double-time, trying to decode that data cube that Claudia got off the raptor," Tane said, his comment catching Cam's attention.

"Heard they have Elle working on it," Levi added.

Cam knew Elle had the best knowledge of the raptor language. She leaned forward. "And the creeper?"

Tane took a sip of his beer. "Bladon's team is keeping it contained so Doc Emerson and her guys can work on it. They're studying it and running tests."

"Hope they can find a way to kill the damn things," Ash said.

"Heard they don't like heat," Tane said.

That the creepers were temperature-sensitive was good to know, but it was also a long way from them finding a way to neutralize the damn things. Cam imagined hordes of the mutated animals rushing through the city, hunting down the last of humanity's survivors. She shuddered, pushing the mental picture away.

She shook her head, and realized her beer was empty. "Another round?"

She got a chorus of yeses, but Ash shook his head and stood. "I'm calling it a night."

"Hot date?" she asked.

A tiny smile. "Something like that."

Levi appeared and slapped a hand on Ash's back. "My friend here is heading back to his quarters to hunch over a damn comp."

Cam frowned. "What?"

"There's a Pre-Emptive Strike tournament tonight," Ash said.

"The computer game?" A laugh burst out of her.

"You do the real thing every day."

"It's kind of cathartic to mow down a bunch of monsters in the game." Ash grinned. "Besides, I'm good. It keeps the geeks on their toes, and they have no idea it's me."

After Ash left, Cam headed over to the bar. She opened the cooler, grabbing several bottles of homebrew out, and popping the tops. Next, she poured another whiskey for Dom.

"He's good, isn't he?"

The female voice made her spin around. "What?" She looked at the woman standing nearby.

She was a few years younger than Cam, with generous curves packed into a tight skirt and a blousy top that showed off a butterfly tattoo over her collarbone. The top also showcased a pair of large breasts, and her pale-brown hair was piled on top of her head.

"Hemi. He rocks in bed, doesn't he?" A smile curved the woman's red lips. "And he can go *all* night." Her eyes got a faraway look in them, and her smile widened.

Cam's gut curdled. She'd known Hemi had a past, but she really didn't want to hear the details. "Is there a reason you feel compelled to tell me this?"

"He's shared his bed with a few of us, and while we all want more, he never comes back for seconds. I just wanted to warn you to enjoy the ride while it lasts."

Cam studied the woman, and didn't detect any malice. This woman's life really revolved around sex, gossip, and by the looks of things, dressing up. Cam blew out a breath. God, when was the last time any of those things had mattered to her? It made her feel ancient. "Look…"

"Tanya."

"Right. This is not a conversation I want to have."

Tanya ignored her. "Hemi loses interest pretty quickly." The woman's gaze flicked over Cam. "Usually he prefers curvy."

Okay, Cam had really had enough. "I think we're done—"

"That man." Tanya made a humming sound. "The other night, when I had my hand on that monster cock of his—"

The other night? A sour taste filled Cam's throat. "What?"

Cam's sharp tone made Tanya blink. The woman took a step back. "Look, I just wanted to warn you. Woman to woman. Enjoy the ride."

Gut churning, Cam spun and marched back to her group. So, Hemi had been chasing Cam and fucking the entire Enclave at the same time. All his pretty words about only being able to think about her… *Ugh*. She slammed the beers down on the table, glass rattling.

She felt Tane watching her and ignored him. She snatched up a beer and took a long swig. They'd made no promises. She'd known whatever the hell this thing was between her and Hemi was short-term. Hell, she'd been pushing him away for months, so she really had no right to feel upset that he'd been fucking pretty, tattooed Tanya.

But he'd made his interest in Cam clear a long time ago. He'd saved her from the alien *oura* mind-control globe, they'd fought side by side numerous times. Dammit, even though she hadn't wanted it to, it had meant something to her.

While it meant something to her, he'd been letting that woman touch him.

Doubts crowded in, panic like acid in Cam's veins. She remembered her mother's paranoia about her father cheating on her. When her father was away, her mother had often forcibly sat Cam down, and ranted and raved about what he might be doing with other women.

Cam had spent years watching her beautiful, confident mother worn down by doubts, fears and uncertainties.

A woman appeared, cocking one hip. "Knew I'd find you guys here."

Indy Bennett was the comms officer for Squad Three. She was in her late twenties, and wore dark jeans, with a tank top the color of blood. She had a silky fall of ink-black hair that she had up in a long ponytail. Her face wasn't quite beautiful, it had too many angles, but it was attractive. The woman had curves that she happily put on display, and beautiful, full-color tattoos that spilled down one arm in a tangle of roses and thorns.

"Indy," Levi called out. "Grab a beer."

The woman shook her head. "The general's called an emergency meeting." Her bright-blue eyes skated across the group. "The tech team decoded the alien cube. You're all going to want to hear what they got off it."

Chapter Eleven

Hemi leaned against the wall in the Command Center. The place was filled with squad leaders and soldiers, and the low rumble of conversation.

Niko and Holmes stood at the front of the room, flanking Elle.

The general rapped his knuckles on the table. The room grew quiet.

"Noah and Elle have decoded the data cube the mission team recovered," Niko announced.

Elle cleared her throat. "Most of the data on the cube references the creepers."

"That's a good thing, right?" Roth called out.

Elle nodded. "What we've learned is that there is a creeper breeding ground."

Grumbles passed through the room. Hemi glanced at Cam. She was standing beside him, but she'd been stiff and distant since they'd left the games room.

"Do we know where it is?" Marcus asked.

"Not yet," Holmes answered. "It describes a vast underground warren."

"We are trying to find a location from the cube data."

"A warren?" Cam murmured.

"You've thought of something?" Hemi asked.

"Sir?" Cam called out. "My squad saw a strange area on a previous mission."

"Yes." Roth shouldered forward. "The ground was pockmarked, like entrances to tunnels."

Elle rushed over to a nearby comp. "I did consider that."

Everybody in the room went quiet. Watching and waiting. Images of the bumpy ground glowing orange filled the room's display screens.

Elle nodded. "At first glance, some elements of the images match the descriptions on the cube." She scanned the crowd, her pretty face tense. "But I can't be a hundred-percent certain that the area that Squad Nine discovered is the creeper breeding ground."

"If the creepers are breeding here," Holmes said, "then we need to stop them."

"We need to confirm it first." Niko shoved his hands in his pockets. "I suggest we find out everything we can about this place, and then decide how to best destroy it."

"Can we send a drone inside it?" Tane asked.

"Risky," Elle said. "It would be noticed easily, in a confined space like this."

A tall, dark-haired man stepped forward. Noah Kim from the tech team. "I have several mini-drones we've been trialing. We could send one in to map this place."

Holmes glanced over their way, his gaze moving to Tane. "Tane, I'm tasking this intel mission to Squad Three."

Hemi watched his brother nod.

Holmes tilted his head. "Get there, take a look around, and deploy the mini-drone." The general's tone turned dry. "And I'd prefer if you didn't engage. Intel-gathering only."

Tane's face stayed noticeably blank. "We'll do our best."

Holmes looked like he wanted to pinch the bridge of his nose. "Be ready to leave at dawn."

When Hemi turned around to talk to Cam, he saw that she'd already left the Command Center.

What the hell? Something was wrong.

As the squads gathered into small groups, talking, Hemi strode out. Stepping into the corridor, he caught a glimpse of her turning a corner at the end of the hall. He broke into a jog and followed.

"Cam?"

She sped up.

"Cam!" He grabbed her arm. "Where's the fire?"

"I have things to do." Her gaze skated to look over his shoulder.

"Me, too. I wanted to talk you into a pre-mission quickie."

He expected a laugh or a joke. Instead, he got a blank face.

"Is that your usual MO? Find a quick fuck?" She tried to pull away. "Find someone else."

What the hell? "Camryn." He gripped her arms and pushed her against the wall. When she shoved at him, he moved closer, pinning her there with his body.

She fought harder. "Get off."

"Not until you tell me what's wrong."

"Screw you."

They scuffled, and finally he grabbed her wrists and slammed them above her head. "Care to explain what the hell is going on in that head of yours?"

She angled her chin. "One of your fuck buddies stopped by for a chat."

Hemi went still. "I wasn't a monk before I met you."

"She told me to enjoy the ride. Apparently, you get bored fast, prefer curves, and the ride won't last very long."

He blinked. She honestly thought that the heat they generated was going to fade. He wanted to laugh, but he saw something in her eyes. "Cam, right now my dick is hard for you and you alone."

"Sure." She pushed against his hold. "I remember my dad telling my mom the same thing loads of times. That she was mistaken, and the other women were all just a misunderstanding."

Ah. The bitterness in her voice was ugly, but Hemi heard the pain under it. He finally felt like he was getting a glimpse under Cam's armor.

"I'm telling you the truth. I don't cheat and I'm sure as hell not your father."

Her lips firmed. "I don't share, Rahia."

He got his face in close to hers. "I don't, either."

"Yeah, right."

Damn, she was stubborn. He opened his mouth to ask more questions when she suddenly moved. A fist was jammed into his side. He grunted, and as he loosened his grip, she spun, trying to escape.

Hell, no. He spun her around, her back pressed to his chest. He wrapped his arms around her, trapping her arms by her sides.

She wriggled and fought, but he waited her out. He didn't want to risk hurting her. Of course, with all her movement, she could hardly miss his hard cock pressed against the curve of her ass.

"Feel that?" He leaned down and nipped the shell of her ear. She tried to jerk her head away. "You did that. No one else."

"So what? You share it around when it suits you."

"What the hell are you talking about, Cam?"

"Tanya said she had her hands on it a few days ago."

Hemi stilled, anger punching through him. But he felt a flash of something else, as well—satisfaction. Cam was jealous.

"That's bullshit. I'm not sure who Tanya is, and I haven't been with anyone since we reached the Enclave."

Cam jerked. "Why would she lie?"

He frowned. "I don't know."

Cam moved, trying to slam her head back into his face.

"Goddammit, Cam!" He tightened his hold. "Why would you believe her over me? You need to talk to me."

"My father always had pretty answers."

It sounded like Cam's parents had done well

fucking up her view of relationships. "Some woman came on to me the other night after dinner. Apparently being a berserker, and having ink and a beard, made her feel like she had the right to try and shove her hand down my pants."

Cam's breaths were coming in sharp pants, but she was listening.

He leaned forward, nuzzling her neck. "The only person I can think of, dream of, and fantasize about is you."

She trembled. "No. We're done. This is done."

His blood ran cold. "Cam—"

"We scratched our itch, Hemi. Let's quit while we're ahead."

He heard the panic in her voice and he snorted. "This is not just fucking, Cam. I told you it's more than that." How long was it going to take him to get that through her thick head?

"No."

He gave a short laugh. "You're jealous. That says it's more."

Cam turned her head, her eyes wide. "I don't get jealous."

He spun her around to face him. "Trust me. Trust *us*. This is the real deal, baby."

She shook her head. "No."

"Trust me," he murmured.

"I…can't." Her voice cracked.

Hemi felt a hot lick of panic and hurt. "You can."

She lifted her chin, and he saw resolve solidify in her eyes. "No. Fucking only, Hemi. You want to fuck, let's fuck."

Her hands went to his belt buckle, yanking him forward. Her lips hit his, hard and angry.

He pulled his head back, his emotions morphing solidly into anger. "God, it's one step forward, ten steps back with you, isn't it?"

She stiffened. "If you—"

He kissed her again, just trying to keep her quiet. "Lucky you're sweet under the fucking toughness, because you'd be a pain in my ass otherwise." He tried to keep the kiss soft, gentle, but like anything with Cam, it turned white-hot.

Hemi knew that he couldn't do this. He couldn't touch her while she thought it was just meaningless sex.

He pulled back. His cock throbbed, begging him to touch her. "I'm not going to do this."

"Fine. You go your way, I'll go mine."

His anger exploded. He grabbed her shoulders and gave her a sharp shake. "Damn you, Cam. I'm done."

Color leached from her face.

"With this conversation." God, she really thought so little of him, felt so little for him. "Fucking hell, Cam, I'm in love with you."

She looked like he'd hit her with a carbine. "No. Don't—"

"I know you don't want to hear it." And fuck, that hurt. "And I know you won't admit that you love me, too. You're afraid. You're letting your past have too much fucking control. You won't trust me and you won't let yourself be vulnerable. I always thought you were the most courageous woman in the world—"

She flinched.

"Now I'm starting to think that maybe you just don't feel enough for me. That I'm not worth it for you."

Her eyes gleamed, a tear sliding down her cheek. "Hemi, I'm sorry."

Damn, she broke his heart. He pulled her close, until their noses brushed. "Don't be sorry, Cam. Be brave. I want you to sort out what you really feel and take a risk…on us."

Then, he let her go and walked away.

***

Cam cut through the water of the Enclave pool.

Stroke, stroke, stroke, breathe. The repetitive moves and the exertion of swimming had always calmed her.

But not today. Today, unruly emotions churned inside her. She'd barely slept. Her damn sheets smelled like Hemi, and, damn the man, she'd missed him. She'd tossed and turned until she couldn't stand being twisted up in her sheets any longer.

It was early and she had the pool to herself, which suited her mood. She stopped at the edge and glanced at the big clock on the wall. She was acutely aware that Squad Three would be getting ready to climb into a Hawk to check out the creeper breeding ground.

Her altercation with Hemi kept running on

repeat through her head. She sagged against the pool edge. She'd accused him of stuff, when she should've just asked him first.

He'd been right. She'd been jealous.

She was so fucked up. Her mother's paranoia and despair, and her parents' poisonous relationship, were never far from her thoughts. And everything else he'd said was true too. She was a coward who was always guarding her heart.

"Hey."

Cam looked up and saw Mac, Taylor, and Sienna standing by the pool.

Ambush.

Cam pulled herself out of the pool to sit on the edge. Her friends sat down beside her—Mac and Taylor cross-legged, and Sienna putting her bare feet in the water. Cam pulled at her black one-piece suit and tossed her goggles onto her towel. She had no idea how they had known she needed them, but as she looked at her friends, she was horrified to feel tears in her eyes.

"Oh, Cam." Sienna threw her arm around Cam's shoulders.

"I fucked up with Hemi. We fought, I accused him of cheating, I keep pushing him away—" Everything poured out of her in a rush. "I don't know why he bothers."

"Because he loves you," Mac said quietly.

Cam gave a watery laugh. "Why?"

"Because you're worth it," Taylor said. "We know you rock and we love you."

Because she was worth it. Cam squeezed her

eyes closed. "He's too good for me."

"You guys are perfect for each other," Sienna insisted. "Too many people just let those berserkers run wild. You stand up to Hemi, challenge him, and rein him in when he needs it."

"That man has worked very hard to run you down," Mac said. "Don't you think it's time you let him catch you?"

"I'm afraid."

"We've all been there," Taylor said. "God, Devlin was terrified of our relationship." The woman smiled. "In a very stoic, British spy way."

"But you never gave up on him," Cam said.

"Because I loved him and I knew that we had something worth fighting for."

"Hemi's never wavered." Not once. Cam swiped at her cheeks. "He's always been there for me, even when I've tried to push him away. I've let fear run my emotions for a very long time."

Mac slapped her back. "Time to dig deep and find some courage, McNab."

Lifting her chin, Cam nodded. Hemi was hers. He deserved to know that he mattered and that... "Oh, God. I'm in love with Hemi."

Her friends laughed, the sound echoing around the pool.

"You just worked that out?" Taylor asked.

"I'm having an emotional crisis here." Cam pressed her palms to her eyes. "Some sympathy and support, please."

"We did that bit," Taylor said dryly. "Now we've moved onto the tough love part."

"Man up," Mac said. "Or woman up, and claim your man."

"And don't ruin the best thing that's ever happened to you," Sienna added with a mock-scowl.

Cam laughed and for the first time in a long time, the chaos inside her eased. She felt threads untangling. She had friends she loved, friends who were the ones who'd shown her the true meaning of family.

She loved Hemi and he loved her. They'd face whatever the future brought together, and kick its butt, just like they did when they fought in a battle.

Mac pushed to her feet. "I'm heading to the Command Center to watch the drone feed of Squad Three's mission." Mac eyed her with a small smile. "Want to join me?"

Cam nodded. "Absolutely. Let me dry off and change." She paused and looked at her friends. "Thank you."

They all smiled and Sienna shot her a saucy wink.

When Mac and Cam entered the Command Center, it was quieter than usual, but the atmosphere was taut. Niko and the general were there. Everyone was intently watching the screens.

She focused on the main video display that showed a feed from the Hawk, the ground flying past as the quadcopter swept in low over the hills. Another screen showed the feed from a camera on Tane's helmet. Cam could see the berserkers in the back of the Hawk, all in their armor and checking their weapons. They were quiet, preparing for their mission.

"Almost at target area," came the disembodied voice of the Hawk pilot. Not Finn today. An older pilot named Robert Kaminski.

Cam spotted Hemi. He was in profile, his face set and serious. For all their wildness, the berserkers didn't always rush into a mission half-cocked.

"We'll do a flyover of the area," the pilot said.

Cam tore her gaze off Hemi and looked at the other screen. Ahead, in the murky morning light, she saw the glow of the breeding ground. She sucked in a breath.

A bad feeling washed over her, causing her skin to itch. She stared at the pockmarked surface and orange glow that made her think of lava. She saw something move, and frowned.

Then, realization struck. The moving shadows were the silhouettes of creepers. They were crawling in and out of the holes. She gasped in a sharp breath.

There were so many of them. Hundreds. *Hell*. All just waiting to be unleashed on the world. As the Hawk circled, she focused on two creatures fighting each other.

"We need more images," Holmes said, nodding at Indy. "Tell them to circle around again."

Indy relayed the order to the pilot, and the Hawk wheeled around in a circle.

"Can you identify the best place to drop us?" Tane's deep voice.

"On it," the pilot said.

Cam's gaze was back on Hemi. She hated that they'd fought, and that he was now out on a mission. Her stomach did a slow roll. *Don't get eaten again, big guy.* Her fingers clenched into her palms, and she suddenly itched for a carbine.

"Shit, what's that?" The pilot's sharp voice. "Evasive maneuvers!"

Cam pushed away from the wall, her pulse spiking. The Hawk suddenly banked hard to the left. The berserkers stumbled and cursed.

"There's another one incoming," the pilot yelled. "What the hell is it?"

"I'm picking up a large heat signature," Indy cried, her fingers flying across her comp screen. "I can't tell what it is!"

"It…it looks like a fireball," the pilot breathed.

Cam saw the mystery object appear on the Hawk's feed—a giant ball of orange. It did look a lot like a fireball.

No, not a fireball. Her breath hitched. "It's a ball of poison. Don't let it—"

"Shit, we're hit," the pilot cried.

The Hawk shuddered and alarms blared. Cam heard the crackle of smashing glass, and an ominous, sizzling sound. She heard the men cursing. Then there was a scream and the sound of rushing wind.

The quadcopter jerked again, and started spinning around in a death spiral. Cam pushed forward, closer to the viewscreens, a sickening sense of dread spreading through her. *No. Pull up. Pull up.*

"Kaminski," Indy said. "Kaminski?" The woman's panicked gaze flicked to the general. "He isn't responding."

"Tell them to brace for impact." Holmes' tone was harsh.

Indy closed her eyes and touched her ear. "Squad Three. Brace for impact."

It happened fast.

On the other screen, Cam saw the ground racing up to meet the damaged Hawk. Hemi. She looked back at his face.

Then the Hawk hit.

There was a deafening crunch of metal, and the screens all went blank.

"Tane? Squad Three?" Indy's voice was frantic. "Respond?"

Nothing.

"Tane, please respond."

Cam stared at the black screens, a horrible emptiness washing through her.

Hemi and his squad had just crashed into the creeper breeding ground.

Chapter Twelve

Cam stroked the smooth surface of her carbine, the vibrations of the Hawk rattling through her tense body. She tapped a boot on the floor. "We there yet?"

"You just asked that a minute ago," Roth said. "Won't be long."

She stared at the gray metal walls of the Hawk, emotions threatening to choke her. *Hemi. God, Hemi.*

"They'll be fine." A hand pressed against her arm, and squeezed. She looked down at Sienna. "He'll be fine."

Cam nodded. "There's no one tougher or luckier than Hemi Rahia."

"That's right. He managed to get you, so he's pretty darn lucky."

"I..." Cam's voice cracked.

Sienna squeezed her arm again. "We'll find them."

Roth appeared on the other side of Cam. "The berserkers are hard to kill."

She nodded, giving her friends a shaky smile. But inside, she knew that they were just men.

Manu was back at base, missing a leg, because he was just a man.

"We're approaching the target zone," Finn called from the cockpit. "I can't risk getting too close, so I'll drop you at the eastern edge of the breeding ground. As close as possible to where the Hawk went down."

Anger vibrated in the pilot's voice. Cam knew the pilots were protective of the quadcopters. They didn't have very many of them, and they were vital in the fight against the Gizzida.

But right now, she was more worried about flesh and blood, than steel.

"Can you see the downed Hawk?" she asked.

"No." Finn's tone was clipped. "No sign of it."

Soon, they hovered a few meters above the ground. Roth swung his carbine off his shoulder. "Let's bring them home."

Cam wasted no time jumping out after Roth. Her squad moved in close, in tight formation, raising their carbines. She scanned their surroundings, drenched in deceptively-pretty morning light. The orange glow from the rough ground ahead was less intense, but it looked no less menacing. There were no signs of any creepers.

There was also no sign of a crashed Hawk.

She frowned, her hands clenching her carbine. Where was it? A quadcopter was hardly tiny.

"Fan out," Roth ordered. "Stay sharp."

Somewhere nearby, a creeper's screech echoed through the air. She stared in the direction of the warren. They were down there. Ready and waiting.

Cam split off with Taylor. They reached the edge of the breeding ground and gingerly stepped onto it. All vegetation had withered and died. The ground was now burned black, dotted with tunnels leading into the ground. It looked like a giant rabbit had burrowed them out. She peered down one tunnel, at the brilliant orange light below.

"Come on," Taylor murmured.

"Squad Nine." Arden's voice in their earpieces. "I can detect hundreds of alien life signs below the ground...but the readings are distorted. It could be more."

More? Great. Cam moved across the barren ground, scanning for the Hawk.

"Arden," Roth said. "I'm deploying the mini-drone now."

"Acknowledged," Arden said. "Lia is on standby to take control of it."

Lia, Finn's better half, ran the drone team. If anyone could get that drone through the tunnels safely, it was Lia.

Cam kept moving. She and Taylor moved across the dead ground, searching. The rest of her squad checked in. No one had found anything.

Nothing. Where was the Hawk? Where were the berserkers? Cam choked back the terrible heavy sensation in her chest. Where was Hemi?

"There's something over there." Taylor nodded off to the right.

They hurried over to the orange glow. Cam's nose wrinkled. The smell was horrible. Both of them stopped at the edge of the pool of orange fluid.

"It's a lake of goo." Taylor's tone matched the look on her face.

Nice. Cam crouched down, snatched up a rock, and tossed it in the fluid. There was no sizzling. She nudged the edge of it with her boot. "It's the same stuff that's in the creeper pods. It isn't poisonous."

That's when Cam saw it. A rotor sticking out of the liquid, several meters away.

Her heart leaped. The Hawk was partly submerged, hidden by some rocks.

"There!" Cam broke into a run.

She and Taylor picked their way across the boggy ground, in some places sinking up to their knees in gunk. Cam could feel it seeping into her boots.

"Watch out for that hole!" Taylor called.

Cam spotted where the goo was bubbling up out of a tunnel entrance. She gave the opening a wide berth, her eye on the twisted metal of the quadcopter.

They got close, rounding some rocks. Cam jerked to a halt at the sight of the shattered cockpit.

The body of the pilot was half hanging out over the glass. *Dammit.* "Roth? Do you copy? We found the Hawk farther west, submerged in the breeding ground." She reached up and pressed a hand to the pilot's bloody neck. "Kaminski's dead."

"Acknowledged." Roth's breathing came over the line, and she knew he'd be moving in their direction. "Any sign of Tane and the others?"

She looked into the fluid-filled Hawk. *God,*

please don't let them have drowned in that stuff.
"No."

Suddenly, she saw movement out of the corner of her eye. She lifted her carbine.

A tattooed arm was reaching up through the fluid beside the Hawk.

"Taylor! Here!"

Cam ran, and skidded to her knees beside the arm. She wrapped her arms around it and started pulling. Taylor arrived a second later, and together they tugged and grunted.

Finally, a big body broke free of the goo, and Ash fell onto dry ground.

He groaned, swiping a hand across his wet face to clear his eyes. His chest was heaving as he sucked in air.

He coughed. "Thanks. The others?"

Cam shook her head. "You're the first we've found. Kaminski didn't make it."

"Fuck." Ash pushed to his feet and pulled his carbine off his shoulder. He swiped his hand over his weapon, sloughing off as much of the goo as he could. "Creepers attacked as soon as we hit. We started fighting."

"Let's find them," Cam said grimly.

Something scary and intense hit Ash's blue eyes. She knew he was considered the prettiest and most charming of the berserkers, and it was sometimes very easy to forget he was just as deadly as the others.

Together, the three of them moved around the downed Hawk. *Where are you, Hemi?* She prayed they hadn't all ended up in the bellies of creepers. God, she wanted to hear his voice, wanted to explain, apologize. She'd pushed him away, claimed she was doing it for him.

But the truth was like a heavy rock in her gut. She'd pushed him away to protect herself. She was so damned terrified of letting a man turn her into what her mother had become.

Her gaze sharpened on a large rock nearby.

She stiffened. No, not a rock. A big body, facedown on the ground. "Found someone!"

They raced over, and as they got closer, she saw long hair brushing the man's shoulders. Levi. He wasn't moving.

"Levi!" Ash dropped down beside his friend, carefully rolling the man over.

Cam watched Ash check the man over with practiced, experienced hands. Her gaze narrowed. They all had combat first responder training, but this looked like more than that.

"There's a contusion on the back of his head." Ash's face was grim.

"Cam, look." Taylor nodded her head.

Footprints, made by combat boots not aliens, lead off across the goop, away from the crash site.

"Ash," Cam said. "Roth and the others are inbound. Stay here with Levi, and then get him to the Hawk. We'll keep looking for the others."

Ash nodded, his blue eyes darkening. "Find them."

"Count on it," Cam answered.

She and Taylor fell into a jog, following the

tracks. In places, they were crisscrossed with what could only be creeper prints. She scanned the ground ahead, hoping for any kind of clue or sign.

All of a sudden, a scraping noise reached her ears. She caught Taylor's gaze and they spun.

Out of a large hole in the ground, a creeper emerged, one scaly leg at a time.

"Did you invite this guy to the party?" Cam raised her carbine.

Taylor did the same. "No, I can't say I did."

"Let's show him how we deal with gatecrashers."

They both opened fire. The alien reared up and screeched.

"Aim for the belly or the mouth," Cam shouted.

The creeper lunged at them, and the women dived and rolled. Cam came up on one knee, still firing. She saw the creeper skittering closer, bringing that sucker mouth far too close for comfort.

"Not today, you ugly bastard." Cam yanked a small frag grenade off her belt. She armed it, then tossed it right at the creeper's mouth.

It sailed right through the jaws.

"Taylor! Take cover." Cam sprinted and dived.

Behind her, she heard a muffled explosion, and then chunks of creeper rained down around her.

"Oh, ew, Cam." Taylor rolled to her feet.

"Gross but effective." She had to admit, she was pretty keen to try that strategy again.

Boots stepped into view and Cam looked up. Roth towered over them. Mac, Sienna, and Theron stood nearby, weapons up.

"Any sign of the rest of Squad Three?" Roth asked.

She shook her head and took his outstretched hand. "Only Ash and Levi. You?"

Her leader shook his head. "Nothing. The mini-drone is mapping the tunnels." He held up his wrist to show her the small screen strapped to it. "So far, no sign of them down there."

"You think they went into the tunnels?" Taylor asked with a grimace.

Cam hoped to hell they hadn't gone into the warren. Her heart felt like a ball of lead in her chest as she scanned their surroundings again.

No one mentioned the possibility that Hemi, Tane, Griff, and Dom were currently ensconced in creeper bellies, but Cam knew that they were all thinking it. The ball in her chest tightened further.

Then she heard something. "What was that?"

Roth frowned. "I didn't hear anything."

Cam hurried over to the tunnel the creeper had emerged from. She cocked her head. Then, the sound came again. It was faint, but discernable. She moved closer. She knew that sound.

She spun. "Carbine fire!"

"Shit." Roth stared into the dark tunnel delving deep into the ground.

Cam kept listening. This time, she heard the unmistakable sound of Hemi's wild laughter.

Her pulse leaped. "They're down in the goddamn warren."

***

143

Hemi lunged forward with his combat knife, fighting the creeper looming over him.

He'd lost his carbine somewhere, but Tane was with him. They fought back to back, his brother firing his carbine.

After the crash, they'd been chased by some creepers, and ended up falling down into one of the mess of tunnels.

The underground warren was a mass of hollowed-out caverns and tunnels. Orange pods covered the walls and floors, tentacles stretching out in all directions. At least the glow of them meant they could see what they were doing.

Nearby, Dom was fighting with his twin knives, fast and deadly. Griff was across the cavern, firing his carbine.

They'd lost Ash and Levi, and Hemi hoped like hell that his mates were okay.

The creeper attacking them let out a deafening screech, its front legs slamming down on either side of Hemi. He jumped up and jammed his knife into the creature's glowing belly. He used his weight to drag the knife down through the skin until it split open, orange fluid splashing over Hemi and the ground.

He rolled through the legs, ignoring the stickiness clinging to him and the shrill cries of the dying creeper.

"Hemi!"

Tane's warning shout had him spinning.

Just in time, he spotted two smaller creepers rushing at him. Damn, they were fast. He dodged, but felt the sharp tip of a leg scrape across his side, tearing a piece of his armor off. It raked his skin and an explosion of pain traveled through him.

The other creeper leaped into the air, aiming for him. These two had to be juveniles, because of their smaller size and lack of bellies. There was only the faintest flush of orange on their abdomens, and they didn't look big enough to swallow him.

But as the creeper descended, Hemi figured it was still going to try. He stabbed up with his knife.

The creeper screeched, its legs curling in as it slammed into the ground beside him. He yanked his knife out.

Then, his leg was pulled out from underneath him and he lost his balance. *Fuck.* The first creeper still had its leg embedded in his armor and skin. It was scrabbling along the tunnel, dragging Hemi along with it.

Damn. If this thing brought him to a larger creeper, he'd be laid out like a feast. And if he got eaten again, Cam would be pissed.

He rolled, the pain turning to agony. He had to get that leg free of him. He hacked at it with his knife but its skin was too fucking hard.

The creeper moved again and his back bumped over the ground. He saw another creeper step into view. A full-sized one, with its sucker mouth opening and closing, its red gaze on Hemi.

Fuck. Fuck. Fuck.

The large creeper moved toward him.

Carbine fire ripped into the creeper. It screeched, skittering backward. The smaller creeper pinning him, jerked under the laser hitting it. Hemi heard shouts and more carbine fire.

He turned his head and watched Cam's lean figure step into view. Her carbine was up, and she was focused on the creeper pinning him.

She was the most beautiful fucking thing he'd ever seen.

The creeper flopped down dead, partially on top of him. Its weight drove the air out of his lungs. *Shit.*

Cam hurried over. She shoved the creeper off him with a grunt. Then she eyed the leg stuck into his side, raised her weapon, and fired. "Hang on." She gripped the remains of the leg and tore it out of him.

Hemi grimaced. She held out a gloved hand and he gripped it. She helped him to his feet.

Her gaze ran over him. "You okay?"

"I am now."

Then she pulled her arm back and landed a hard punch to his gut. He doubled over.

"Do not scare me like this again," she said.

He lifted his head and grinned. "Hey, I'm injured. I was just about to thank you for rescuing me. I thought I did a pretty good damsel impression."

This time, she shook her head, pulled him forward and kissed him.

"That's better," he murmured against her lips. The taste of Cam was enough to wash all the pain, filth, and sweat away.

Squad Nine surrounded them, scaring off the

remaining creepers lurking at the far end of the cavern.

"Save that for later," Mac called out.

"Let's get out of here." Cam raised a brow. "Unless you're enjoying playing with the creepers, and want to stay a little longer?"

Hemi pulled her close. "I can think of other things I'd prefer to play with more."

A loud screech echoed out of a side tunnel. A chorus of howls answered it.

Hemi's shoulders tensed. That sounded like a hell of a lot of those damn monsters.

"Let's go, people," Roth called out.

They moved in closer, and headed toward the tunnel Squad Nine had used to get down there. Hemi was eager to get back to the Enclave. He wanted a hot shower, a cold beer, and Cam. Not necessarily in that order.

Suddenly, he felt the floor bow beneath his weight. He stopped.

"Hemi?" From two steps ahead of him, Cam turned and frowned.

He stared down suspiciously at the gooey orange surface beneath his boots. A second later, the ground gave way.

Hemi dropped, falling into a pool of orange fluid with a splash. He looked up...just in time to see a grate slide closed across the opening, just above his head. Trapping him.

"Aw, *fuck.*"

Chapter Thirteen

"Hemi!"

The shout ripped painfully from Cam's throat. She dropped down on her knees, and stared down through the grate covering the hole Hemi had fallen into.

She gripped the lattice—it was made of some sort of bone-like substance. Below, Hemi bobbed, chest-deep in fluid.

He reached up, wrapping one hand over hers. "I'm okay."

Cam squeezed his fingers. "Hold tight. We'll get you out." She looked over her shoulder. "A little help here?"

A second later, Tane and Roth dropped down beside her.

"Bro, we'll get you out in a sec," Tane said.

Both men, together with Cam, yanked on the bone grate. It didn't budge. Cam tried to work the end of her carbine in to try and pry it off. No movement.

"There are more of these hidden holes around here," Mac called out. She was probing the ground with her carbine. "They look like some sort of trap."

Cam scanned the room. She guessed the creepers chased their prey in here, and trapped them down in these fluid-filled chutes.

Cam yanked her combat knife out and tried to hack away at the bone. She let out a grunt of frustration. It was too damn tough.

"We have more creepers incoming," Taylor called out. She was standing near a tunnel entrance.

"Buy us some time," Roth ordered.

As one, Taylor, Theron, and Sienna moved forward to engage the incoming creepers. Carbine fire echoed loudly around them.

With a horrible feeling trickling through her chest, Cam grabbed the bone grate again and heaved with all her strength.

"Shit."

Hemi's quiet mutter made her look down at him. Through the grate, their gazes locked.

"What's wrong?" she asked.

"I can feel suction in the fluid."

She swallowed. "What?"

His gaze moved over her face. "It's trying to suck me down."

Her fingers tightened on the grate. "You hold on."

Cam watched as Hemi's body snapped tight, like someone was pulling on his feet. His knuckles turned white.

No. No. No. "Don't you damn well leave me, Rahia. Hold on." She couldn't lose him. She started pulling at the grate like a wild woman. "Move, damn you!"

"Cam." His quiet tone made her look at him. "I love you."

She sucked in a quick breath. "No. Don't say it like that!"

One of his big, blunt fingers moved a centimeter to brush hers. "Baby."

Cam's emotions tore at her, shredding her insides. She pressed her hand over his. "I love you, too, Rahia. I'm scared spitless, and I know I'll screw this up—"

"You aren't your mom or your dad, Cam. You're way stronger and way more honorable."

A tear slid down her cheek. God, now she was crying. "Don't talk like this is goodbye."

"You have so much love and passion locked inside you. Use it." Suddenly, a grimace crossed his face.

Then, his hold on the grate was torn away, and he was sucked downward. Horrified, she saw his dark head disappear down into the goo.

"No! Hemi!" She kept tearing at the bone grid, trying to get it to move. Her hands stung beneath her gloves, layers of skin tearing off her palms.

Strong arms wrapped around her and pulled back.

"No! I have to get to him. No!"

She kept staring at that dark hole where he'd disappeared, terrified that the moment she looked away, he would be gone forever. The truth crept into her throat like a bitter poison. He was gone. She kept struggling. He was gone.

"Cam? Cam?" Hands grasped her arms, and she

was spun around. She stared blankly into Roth's set face. "Concentrate."

"He's gone." A voice filled with pain cracked through the words.

She looked over at Tane. Hemi's brother was staring at the hole too, the scariest look she'd ever seen on his face.

"We have to find him," she said.

Tane's eyes met hers—a terrible look in them. He nodded.

Roth squeezed Cam's arm. "We don't leave anyone behind." He tilted his wrist, looking at the screen. "The mini-drone has been busy mapping the tunnels. I think we can work out where this trap comes out."

With a plan of attack in place, Cam managed to clear her head and focus. Hemi needed her. She couldn't fail him. Beside her, Mac leaned in and gave her a brief hug.

Roth's brow creased. "I need to tell you all that the lower levels of the warren are crawling with creepers. We are seriously outnumbered and the likelihood of mission success is low."

Cam lifted her chin. She didn't give a crap about odds. She was going to get Hemi.

She looked around at her squad. They all lifted their weapons.

"We getting this show on the road, or what?" Theron rumbled.

They stood with her and her man. Cam fought back a mass of emotions. Their support meant the world to her, and reminded her that she wasn't alone. She was surrounded by honorable people. People with grit who never gave up. She looked up and her gaze locked with Tane's.

They would get him back. She had to find the man she loved.

Love. She swallowed a few times and locked that away for later. When they were safe and she could hyperventilate in peace.

Carbine fire sounded in a nearby tunnel.

"Someone's coming," Sienna shouted.

A big body rolled out of a tunnel. Ash leaped to his feet and faced them. "God, I've been looking everywhere for you guys."

"Levi?" Tane asked.

"On the Hawk with Finn. Out cold with a head injury."

"He'll be pissed he missed this," Griff said in a low, gruff voice.

"Hemi got sucked down some creeper trap," Tane said.

Cam lifted her carbine. "We're going to find him."

Ash nodded, swinging his own carbine around. From the shiny, unscratched surface of it, Cam guessed it was a spare he'd grabbed off the Hawk. He also had two bulky backpacks slung on each shoulder. "I brought some extra weapons. Levi will be *really* pissed he missed the fun." A sexy smile. "I'll enjoy rubbing his face in it."

They all huddled over Roth's map. "We're here." Roth pointed to a glowing point. "Looks like all these tubes are traps. They lead straight down over to this area." He pointed to another spot in the maze of breeding ground tunnels. "By the size of it, some sort of large cavern below."

"How do we get down there?" Cam asked.

She tried not to think about Hemi. He'd already been gone too long. Drowning in that horrid gunk. *Hold it together.* The bad thoughts wouldn't help him. Besides, this was Hemi they were talking about. The man had nine lives.

"There." Tane pointed with one long finger to a sloping tunnel behind them. "This seems to be the most direct route down to this larger cavern."

"Agreed," Roth said. "Let's move out."

Tane took one of the packs from Ash, slipping into the shoulder straps. He tightened it, and then unhooked some sort of hose from the side of the pack. Beside him, Ash was doing the same thing.

"What's that?" she asked.

Tane gave her a tiny, but very scary, smile. "You'll see. Ready?"

She nodded, and the rest of her squad nodded as well.

They started toward the tunnel. The opening gaped like some demon's mouth, waiting to swallow them whole.

Not today. Cam knew that Hemi wouldn't give up on her. He'd been an unstoppable force, battering at her until she gave in to him. And he was right, she wasn't her parents. She couldn't see either one of her parents risking their comfort or safety, let alone their lives, for the other.

Be alive, Hemi. She lifted her carbine and

stepped into the sloping tunnel. "Let's go rescue my man."

***

Hemi's lungs burned, his body scraping against rock, as he was sucked down through the tunnel.

Everything in him screamed for him to open his mouth and take a breath. He struggled not to, but as the pressure in his lungs increased, he lost the fight.

His mouth opened and the alien fluid ran down his throat, choking him.

He thrashed around, but before he could think about dying, suddenly he was flying through the air. He smacked into the ground and rolled a few times.

He came to a stop, flopping on his stomach. *Fuck.* He coughed up goo until his muscles cried from heaving so much.

A noise made him raise his head.

He saw two creepers just a few meters away, watching him. *Great.* He reached down to the sheath on his thigh and realized his combat knife was gone. He had no weapons.

He studied the creepers again. They weren't moving. They looked like statues. He glanced around. This cavern was larger, and there were pods dotted around the walls and floor in here, too. He squinted. These pods looked different. They were larger, more circular. In the closest one, he saw something move. A shadow with lots of legs.

He went still. It was a *creeper* inside. All these pods were growing creepers. So where had these pods come from?

A deep rumble echoed through the cavern. The two creepers that had been watching him turned, and scuttled off into the darkness.

A shadow moved at the far end of the cavern, detaching from the wall.

Fuck me. Hemi's jaw dropped. A massive creeper, the size of a truck, advanced. The damn thing towered over him, and all the other creepers.

The big motherfucker's red eyes zeroed in on Hemi. *Great, just great.* Apparently, it was "don't give Hemi a break" day.

Not that he was giving up.

"Come on, asshole." Hemi pushed to his feet. "I finally have the woman I love, who has given me a hell of a run-around, where I've been dreaming of having her. So if you think I'm going to stand here and quake in my boots and let you eat me for breakfast, well...fuck you."

The giant creeper paused and tilted its ugly head, studying Hemi like something strange but tasty.

Then it charged.

Holy fuck. Hemi rushed beneath it, dodging giant legs. Its huge orange belly glowed overhead, well out of reach.

Come on, Hemi, think. He needed a weapon and a plan.

The creeper spun and Hemi ducked through the legs again. Lacking a plan, he was happy to make a run for it. He spotted a tunnel entrance, but it was on the far side of the cavern.

Only a giant alien creeper between him and the exit. No problem.

A giant leg slammed into Hemi, sending him airborne. He hit the ground and rolled. When he looked up, the leg was rushing down at him.

Hemi rolled to the side. *Bam*. The leg struck the ground where his head had been a second before. The creeper let out a furious screech and drew back, aiming again.

Hemi rolled to the other side. *Bam*. Rock chips peppered his face.

Damn. He leaped to his feet and ran, his gaze focused on the tunnel.

A giant force slammed into him, lifting him off his feet. The creeper had caught him with a different leg this time. He flew through the air and slammed into the rock wall.

He fell in a heap, the air knocked out of him and pain tearing through him.

Shit, he'd broken a rib or two. He ignored the pain and pushed himself up, his fingers brushing over something hard on the ground. The bone of some animal.

He grabbed it and leaped to his feet, belatedly realizing that there were piles of bones around him. The traps leading down here had to be ways to feed the queen creeper. He hefted the bone, brandishing it in front of him.

The creeper was coming at him again. Its huge sucker mouth was large enough to swallow a car, and it was heading straight for Hemi.

He darted around the side of the creature. He was faster and more nimble than this creeper, so he needed to use that to his advantage.

One huge leg slammed down right in front of him. He stared at the inky-black scales for a second, then grabbed it. Quickly, he shimmied up the leg. As he neared the creature's back, it tried to shake him off, but Hemi clung to it.

Staying alive, getting back to Cam, depended on him not losing his grip.

He pulled himself onto the back of the creeper. He ran along its back, its body shifting under him, heading for the beast's head. He lifted the bone high above himself.

Without stopping, he jammed the bone into the creeper's eyes.

It let out a deep screech—filled with pain and anger. It bucked and spun wildly, and Hemi went flying.

He slammed into a pod, before dropping to the floor. He looked up to see the agitated creature shaking its head, trying to dislodge the bone.

Time to go.

He glanced over and saw that, for once, he'd gotten a break. He was right near the tunnel leading out of here. He headed that way, limping around the pods.

As he neared the tunnel entrance, a creeper appeared, skittering out of the tunnel.

Aw, shit. Hemi paused. After taking on a giant-ass creeper, surely one regular one should be a breeze.

But then another stepped out of the darkness behind the first. And another and another.

Shit. His jaw tightened. One creeper, he could manage, but a whole pack of them...

He backed up a few steps and bumped into a pod. He felt it vibrate, and looked down to see the top of it unfurling, like some monstrous flower.

As he watched, a black, scaly leg poked its way up out of the pod, covered in sticky orange goo.

No fucking break for Hemi. Grimly, he faced the creepers coming out of the tunnel. He thought of Cam.

He didn't want to leave her, and whatever happened, however many aliens were tossed his way, he'd go down fighting. She'd know he fought to get back to her.

One of the creepers pounced forward, landing right near him. He ran and slid in beneath it, like he was trying to steal a base. He punched up into its belly. It staggered. He gripped one of its back legs and pulled hard. Damn, they were tough. With thoughts of Cam in his head, he heaved, straining with every ounce of his strength.

He heard something snap, and the creature let out a vicious screech.

Hemi backed away from the injured creeper. A rushing sound caught his ear, and he turned to see a second creeper darting toward him. He dodged it, but one of its legs hit him, knocking him down.

He struck the ground, just as a third creeper reared up over him. It brought down one of its legs, and skewered him through his shoulder, pinning him to the ground. Hemi roared in pain.

The creeper lowered its hungry mouth, and in its demonic eyes, Hemi saw wild, raging hunger.

Then it stopped and shrieked. It yanked its leg out of him, and turned around with another wild screech. Hemi groaned, feeling blood pulsing out of the wound. With surprise, he realized one of the other creepers had attacked the one that had been about to devour him. They were fighting over him like he was some kind of juicy bone.

As the two creepers battled, their forelegs snapping against each other, Hemi scooted backward. He pressed a palm to his shoulder, and his hand came away drenched in blood. But he kept his gaze on the creepers. This could be his last chance to sneak out.

As he turned around to make his escape, another creeper was looming over him from behind.

"Come on then, motherfucker," he shouted.

The creature came closer, opening its giant mouth.

Suddenly, a wave of flames rushed over them. Hemi dived, rolled, and buried his face in his arms. He felt the hot wave sear his back, and the creepers' high-pitched screeching filled the cavern.

"Take that, assholes."

Tane's voice. Hemi raised his head, and spotted Tane and Ash holding flamethrowers.

Both men looked completely relaxed, and hell,

Ash was even grinning. They were methodically sweeping the flamethrower hoses back and forth. Fire rushed over the creepers and the pods. Some of the pods burst open, new creepers pouring out.

Behind his squad mates, Hemi saw soldiers rush forward. Carbine fire lit up the room, joining the orange flames.

Cam was leading her squad, firing at anything that moved.

Hemi smiled, pulling himself up to lean against the rock wall. There was his woman—beautiful and deadly.

Chapter Fourteen

The smell of burning flesh was sharp in Cam's nose, and the screeches of the dying creepers rang in her ears.

The rest of her squad was exterminating the remaining creepers in the cavern, but she only had eyes for one thing. One man.

She leaped over a pod and rushed over to Hemi. He stood slumped against the wall, a grin on his face.

"God, Hemi." As she reached him, his legs went out from under him. She wrapped her arms around him, trying to keep him upright. The guy was built like a tank. She lowered them both to the ground and tightened her hold on him. "You look terrible."

He was covered in blood and orange gunk. His face was pale under his dark beard, and lines of pain bracketed his eyes.

He grinned at her through the gore. "Hey, baby."

He was smiling. Idiotic moron. She knew that was redundant, but it seemed to apply. "I...I..." Tears threatened.

"Hey." He reached up and cupped her cheek.

"I love you, damn you."

His grin widened. "I know."

She pressed her forehead to his. "I thought you were gone. It scared me more than anything."

"I'm pretty tough to kill."

She gave a hiccupping laugh. "Like a cockroach?"

He barked out a laugh, but it quickly turned to a grimace. She spotted his bloody shoulder, and quickly yanked open the field med kit on her belt. She pressed absorbent gauze to the ugly injury. Damn creepers, she wanted to kill every one of them with her bare hands.

Hemi ignored her hands as she tended his wound, his gaze on her face. "I've been waiting forever for you to be mine. I love you, Camryn."

She went still, her heart bursting. "I'm still afraid. I'm afraid that I'll screw up, that you'll screw up, that I'll drive you away or lose you."

"There aren't any guarantees," he said.

"I don't ever want us to look at each other the way my parents looked at each other. With so much poison and hate." If that happened to her and Hemi...no, she wouldn't be able to live with it.

His hand gripped hers, moving it a few inches from his wound until her palm was pressed over his beating heart. "It's like when you pick up your carbine and step into a fight. Every day, we do, not knowing if we'll win, or if we'll make it back. You've just got to believe that the reason you're doing it is worth it."

Something in Cam stilled and went quiet. "You're worth it."

His hands tightened on her. "*We're* worth it."

"Time to go." Roth stepped up beside them. "There are several thousand more creepers in here and I think we've overstayed our welcome."

Cam pressed her shoulder in under Hemi's arm.

Tane moved in front of them. "I know this was supposed to be a recon mission—" He pulled some things from the backpack on his shoulder. "—but I brought a few extra toys with me."

Cam recognized the small, silver devices. Each had two tiny windows on it. One showed a line of glowing blue and the other a line of glowing red. When the two lines met...well, it was best not to be around when that happened.

Roth shook his head. "All right. Let's move out."

Cam helped Hemi toward the tunnel. Her squad moved to take point, carbines up. Behind them, Griff and Dom brought up the rear, while Tane and Ash moved around the cavern, setting the charges.

As they hobbled into the tunnel, Tane and Ash jogged up to join them. Tane slipped an arm around his brother to help take his weight.

"We're going to make a little mess for our friends to deal with," Tane murmured.

"Nice," Hemi replied.

Cam rolled her eyes.

As a group, they headed up the ramp. Roth led them through the tunnels' twists and turns, a few creepers attacking and easily dealt with.

"Roth? Large..." Arden's distorted voice. "...creepers converging."

Roth touched his ear. "Arden, say again?"

"More...too many."

Static filled the line.

Screeches echoed through the tunnels around them. From all the tunnels.

Cam tightened her hold on Hemi and Tane stepped away, lifting his flamethrower hose.

"Just can't get a fucking break today," Hemi grumbled.

"Creepers!" someone shouted.

Cam watched her squad and the berserkers turn to face the incoming aliens. God, there were so many of them.

She heard more sounds coming from the tunnel behind them. *Shit.* Her jaw tightened and she moved to lean Hemi against the wall. She needed to protect him—

"Hell Squad, ready to go to hell?" a deep voice yelled.

"Hell yeah," came several voices, echoing off the rock walls. "The devil needs an ass kicking!"

Hell Squad sprinted out of the tunnel, carbines firing.

"Looks like you caught a break after all, Rahia," Cam said.

He let out a laugh but she could tell he was in pain. "Well, you finally admitted you loved me, so it is my lucky day after all."

Cam leaned into him and watched as the Hell Squad soldiers barreled into the fight with the others. Within minutes, the creepers were all down.

"Nice of you to join us, Steele," Roth said. "*After* we rescued Squad Three and practically fought our way back out all by ourselves."

Marcus raised a brow. "You're welcome, Masters."

"The general thought you guys might need a hand," Cruz said, studying the maze of tunnels around them. "And we are here for clean up."

"You get the berserkers out of here," Marcus said. "We're going to assess the breeding ground and how best to destroy it."

"We already set some explosives," Ash said. "In the queen's cavern below."

"Send me the data." Marcus held up his wrist and Cam saw he had a screen identical to Roth's. "We'll add what we brought with us and bring the entire place down."

Roth nodded. "Have fun."

Shaw grinned, his sniper rifle resting on his shoulder. "Blowing up aliens is always fun."

Soon, Tane was back to help Cam with Hemi and they were headed for the surface. She felt a rush of fresh, clean air, and relief surged. They were almost out.

Roth stood at the entrance, waving them forward. "Everyone, let's move back to the Hawk as fast as you can."

Cam looked up into the bright-blue sky overhead. "We're heading home, big guy."

"Good. I have plans." He waggled his eyebrows.

"Yes, a trip to Medical," she said dryly.

"Watch out!"

At Ash's shout, Cam glanced over. A juvenile creeper rushed up behind them. Ash leaped on top of it, stabbing it with his combat knife.

165

The creeper spun wildly, and alien and man crashed into a rock wall. There was a shimmer of light, and the wall blinked out of existence.

Cam controlled a gasp. Behind it was a space filled with raptor comp screens and a humming alien generator.

Holographic camouflage. She'd heard of the raptors using it to hide their tech.

Ash killed the juvenile, jumped off it, and gripped it by a leg. With a giant heave, he tossed it out of the away. Then he straightened and stared at the comp screens. "Look at that."

"What is it?" Tane called out.

Ash stepped up to the screens, and nudged a pile of raptor data cubes with his boot. "My guess? This is this is some sort of control station for the breeding ground." He picked up a slick black cube. "Could have good data on the creepers."

"Grab the cubes," Tane ordered.

With a nod, Ash opened a backpack and scooped the cubes into it.

Tane touched his earpiece. "Indy, we found some raptor cubes. Relay a message to Hell Squad to keep an eye out for any more."

Cam couldn't care less about raptor cubes or creepers. With Hemi's warmth pressed against her side, she didn't want to think about aliens for at least the next twenty-four hours.

"Let's go home," she murmured to Hemi.

***

Hemi let Tane take most of his weight to help him aboard the Hawk. He actually was feeling much better now, but he was pretty sure that was just because he had Cam, his brother, and his friends by his side.

He dropped down into a seat and winced at the pain in his ribs. Cam sat beside him, but before she could settle, he yanked her into his lap.

"Hemi, your ribs—"

"Are fine. Stay still." She froze and he pressed his face to her neck. "Holding you is worth any pain."

She made a small sound and settled into him.

"I need a beer, shower, and a hard fuck," Hemi said.

Chuckles broke out around them, and Cam lifted her head and rolled her eyes. "Well, I hope the shower is first on the list. You smell bad."

"He won't look much better after a shower," Ash called out. "You sure you want to hang out with him, Cam?"

"Quit flirting with my woman, Connors." Hemi tightened his arms around a smiling Cam. "I feel on top of the fucking world. I'm alive and my woman, the sexiest most beautiful badass ever, loves me."

"A bit louder, Rahia," she said. "I don't think the Gizzida heard you."

He cupped the back of her head and pulled her in for a kiss. A slow, thorough kiss.

"I love you too, you Neanderthal."

"The backfire explosives are going," Ash called out.

Hemi turned to look out the window.

Boom. The Hawk vibrated, and outside, he saw a huge blue ball rise into the air. Then the heart of it turned a brilliant red. Hell Squad did not mess around.

He had no idea how big the damn creeper breeding grounds were, but he knew they had to have caused a fuckload of damage.

"What did I miss?" a groggy voice asked.

They all turned to see a dazed Levi sitting up on his stretcher in the back of the Hawk, his long hair brushing his shoulders.

Laughter broke out, and Ash moved over to check his friend.

"Mate, you kind of missed everything." Ash probed Levi's head wound.

Levi groaned. "Great. And you'll never let me live it down."

Hemi held onto Cam, and listened to the murmurs of his squad and Squad Nine around him. He'd meant what he'd said to Cam earlier. Each time they stepped onto a Hawk, they never knew if they'd make it back from the mission. There were no guarantees, but what they did was important, and every risk was worth it.

Hemi had always lived by his own rules. It was part of the reason he'd never joined the military. Working as a mercenary had let him pick his own fights. The ones that suited him and his own beliefs.

But sitting here, with these brave men and women, and holding the woman he loved in his arms, he knew he'd go out there every hour of every day to fight the aliens. For these people, for the people at the Enclave, for Cam, he'd take on every alien he could find until they were all gone. Because what he had right here was worth fighting for.

"Ladies and gentlemen, welcome home," Finn called out from the cockpit.

The Hawk stopped, hovered for a moment, then started to descend. They landed in the hangar, and when Roth pushed back the door, the first thing Hemi saw was Doc Emerson waiting with two stretchers.

Aw, shit. Ash and Tane quickly loaded a still-groggy and complaining Levi onto a stretcher. Hemi warily stepped down from the Hawk, holding on tightly to Cam.

The doc looked at him and rubbed her hands together. "I've been looking for some more victims today." She pointed to the stretcher.

Hell, no. "I can walk—"

"Climb aboard, Rahia. I promise to only stick you with needles once or twice." Emerson pursed her lips, her critical gaze running over him. "Actually, it might be a few more than that."

"Cam can help me—"

"Up," Emerson said.

"I need a shower—"

The doctor shook her head, her blonde hair fluttering against her jaw. "From what I can tell, you have a still-bleeding wound to your shoulder, some other scrapes and cuts, and my guess is you've likely broken some ribs. Plus, I heard you nearly drowned in alien fluid, so I need to check you out." Her eyes hardened. "And you've pulled the shower thing on me before, Hemi. It took me two to days track you down last time."

Cam shot him an amused look. "Not afraid, are you?"

"Afraid?" He made a scoffing noise.

"Then get on the stretcher, Hemi," Cam said.

He hesitated. He fucking hated needles, but there was no way he was admitting that.

Cam leaned in, her lips pressed to his ear. "I'll make it worth your while," she murmured.

He looked at her. "Oh yeah? With what?"

"Dirty sexual favors."

"In that case…" Hemi pulled himself up on the stretcher.

As they headed out of the hangar, Cam's full-throated laugh made him smile.

Chapter Fifteen

Ash

Ash Connors carried the bag of alien data cubes down the corridor leading to the tech lab.

Most people would be heading to the dining room for dinner, but he knew one of the geeks would still be in the lab, tinkering with something or hunched over a comp screen. He was in desperate need of a shower. He was still in his armor and covered in alien fluid, sweat, and blood, but he wanted to deliver these cubes first.

God, he was tired. He was weary down to his bones. Most days, it felt like they were always fighting. Ash had never been averse to wading into a fight—when he'd been a kid raised by a rough biker dad, when he'd been Levi's second-in-command of the Iron Kings, or as a berserker fighting invading aliens.

But right now, tired, aching, and smelling like alien shit, it was hard to remember why he was fighting.

He kicked open the door. A woman jerked in her chair and spun around, blonde curls bobbing.

"Sorry," he grunted.

Her gaze slid over him, her eyes widening. "Uh...hi."

He lifted his chin and moved over to a long bench. He upended the bag and cubes dropped down onto the surface.

"Watch out!" The blonde rushed over, nudging him out of the way. "This is delicate equipment here. And you shouldn't be tossing the cubes around. You might break them."

Her snarky tone was somewhere between scolding teacher and pissed-off woman. Ash looked down at the top of her head. He couldn't remember the last time a woman had told him off.

Usually, they got all breathy and fluttered their eyelashes. Or they were fellow soldiers talking in no-nonsense words.

The woman righted the cubes with small hands. She was pretty short compared to him.

"Thought you'd want these right away," he said.

She glanced up at him with annoyed, clear blue eyes. Then she clearly realized her nose was an inch from his blood-splattered armor, and she backed up a step.

She was cute. Ash had always had a thing for cute.

"Thanks," she mumbled reluctantly. "Where did you find them?"

"In an underground creeper breeding ground we just blew sky-high."

Those eyes widened again. But there was no fear or shock, just intelligence and interest. "Wow." She picked up one of the cubes, turning it over.

And then it was like he didn't exist. She stared at the cube, and then snatched up another one. It looked like she'd forgotten he was even in the room.

Ash wasn't used to that, either. He knew he was attractive. Ever since he'd hit puberty, the opposite sex had been interested, starting with a much older cheerleader who'd divested him of his virginity. He was used to women showing him attention.

But this little tech geek seemed oblivious, and he didn't like that. He moved closer, crowding into her space, and instantly he smelled her. Fresh, clean woman, with a hint of something that made him think of a bunch of sunny flowers.

"We'll see what we can get off them." She went still and scowled at him. "You're too close."

"I'm not touching you."

"That's not the point." She shot daggers at him. "It's good manners not to invade someone's personal space."

He smiled at her. "Manners aren't really my thing."

Her gaze dropped to his lips and she blinked. Then she slid sideways between Ash and the bench to reach her comp. She clicked the data cube into a small cradle.

Information flickered up on the screen. She leaned forward. "Cool. My raptor isn't that great, but this looks like creeper info. Noah and the others will *love* this."

Yep, she'd forgotten he was there again. Luckily, Ash had a pretty healthy ego. He let his gaze slide down her figure. She was wearing a long, flannel shirt over jeans, which made it hard to tell much about what she looked like underneath. But as she leaned over, the shirt hiked up enough for him to note a curvy little ass encased in denim.

He watched as her slim fingers flew across the keyboard and tapped on the screen.

"It has some heavy-duty encryption on parts of the data." She muttered under her breath. "You can't keep me out...gotcha!" She stepped back and wiggled her hips in a little victory dance. Then she realized he was still there, and stiffened.

He smiled. Her face was flushed, satisfaction sparkling in her eyes.

"Oh," she said. "Are you still here?"

He folded his arms over his chest. "Yep."

Her gaze skated over his arms. He and the rest of his squad rarely wore armor on their arms. She lingered on his tattoos for a long moment, before jerking her attention back to the comp screen.

His cute little geek was noticing him now.

She cleared her throat and touched a key. The alien information disappeared. An image from a computer game blinked onto the screen. A squad of armored soldiers appeared to be fighting their way through monsters.

"You play Pre-Emptive Strike?" he asked.

"A lot of people in the base do." She hunched her shoulders. "Is this where you ridicule me, and all the other nerds?"

"No."

She eyed him warily. "I'm sure a badass soldier like you doesn't play war games."

Ash raised a hand and pointed to the carbine on his shoulder. "I've got the real thing."

She swallowed, and he watched her slim throat work. "Right."

He leaned down and lowered his voice. "But you'd be surprised what games a badass soldier like me enjoys playing."

She stared at him, her lips parting.

He smiled at her. Yep, she was cute as hell. He watched her gaze slide down to his lips. "Good night, Marin."

Now her gaze jerked up to his. "You know my name?"

Ash smiled again and turned. As he headed out of the tech lab, he didn't feel so tired anymore. Apparently, teasing Marin Mitchell was more energizing than a hot shower and a beer.

***

"Oh yes, Hemi. God, harder."

Hell. Hemi leaned back in the armchair, his hands gripping the armrests. A naked Cam was on his lap, bouncing up and down on his cock. He was busy watching her face—studying every flicker of emotion that crossed her beautiful features.

"Take me, Cam," he growled. He felt his climax growing, clamping down on his muscles.

"I am," she panted.

He let go of the armrests and gripped her hips, helping to work her up and down. Faster. Harder. Her eyelashes fluttered closed.

"Eyes, Cam," he demanded.

Her eyes opened and her gaze met his. Two more thrusts and she came, crying out his name.

A second later, he yanked her hips down, holding her there and grinding against her as he came.

She collapsed against his chest, her face pressed to his shoulder. "I can't move. Maybe in a year or two. Definitely a decade."

He stroked a hand down her slim back. Her skin was slick with perspiration. Finally, she was his. He breathed in the scent of her. Finally, he had his everything.

He'd survived his trip to Medical, and he'd been more than happy to let Cam fuss over him. The needles had sucked, but afterward, he'd rushed Cam back to her room for dirty sexual favors. That bit definitely hadn't sucked.

"I feel safe with you."

Her words were so quiet that Hemi almost missed them. He went still, his palm pressed to her spine. He knew what that confession meant to her.

He lifted her face, cupping her cheeks. "I will never cheat on you, and I will spend every day showing you how much I love you. Your mind, your body, and your attitude."

Her gaze narrowed. "I don't have any attitude."

He grinned at her. "Yeah, baby, you do. And I love it." Then his smile melted away. "I'll never leave you, and if I'm not by your side, I'll fight to get back there. Where I belong."

"Hemi." Her face went soft. "For a tough,

tattooed badass, you say some pretty sweet things." She grinned. "But I'll keep your secret."

He tilted his head.

"That you're just a big teddy bear under the badass."

He reached behind her and slapped her butt playfully. "Watch it, McNab."

She laughed, that full-throated, sexy laugh that he loved.

"Now, put something sexy on," he told her. "We're off to movie night."

She climbed off him and strode into the bathroom to wash up. Soon she was back, fishing around in her closet. He stared at her long, naked body and his damn cock stirred.

"What are we watching?" she asked.

Your luscious legs. He shook his head. Instinctively, he knew that even when he was old and gray, he'd still want this woman. "A classic. About an alien that gets loose on a ship. You know, that one where the alien bursts out of someone's stomach."

Cam pulled on some underwear and glanced his way. "Well, I guess that's better than one where some idiot gets swallowed whole by an alien and ends up in the alien's stomach."

He'd never live that one down. He watched her dress, amazed that he loved the small things just as much as the big ones. Watching her dress, smile, walk, hell...he could watch her just breathing and be happy.

She stepped into some tight jeans and wiggled

her hips to get them into place. Hemi was getting less and less interested in watching a movie.

"You'd better get back to your place, and get dressed," she said. "Or we'll be late."

"I want to move in."

At his words, she paused in fastening her jeans. Then, she smiled at him. "I think I'd like that."

She hadn't even flinched. Progress. Hemi stood and yanked on his own jeans. He pressed a quick kiss to her bare shoulder. "Good. I love you."

The faintest twitch of her eye. "I love you, too."

"I'll see you at movie night. Don't be late."

***

Cam sauntered down the corridor toward the rec room, trying not to whistle. Damn, she was happy.

They'd survived the mission, rescued Squad Three, and dealt a significant blow to the creeper breeding grounds.

Oh, she knew it wasn't the end. Knew the Gizzida would be regrouping, that they'd have more breeding grounds elsewhere, and would no doubt retaliate. But for now, with her body still relaxed from some delicious, sexy loving, she was going to just enjoy the buzz.

She turned the corner and spotted General Holmes ahead, one palm pressed against the wall. Shock was stamped all over his aristocratic face.

"General? Adam?" Cam rushed over to him. She'd never seen the man so rattled. She'd watched him face Gizzida attacks, alien creatures, and death. He'd always been a stoic man, the strong leader they needed to face everything that had been thrown at them. "What's happened? Is the research on the creeper not going well? God, it didn't get loose, did it?"

"No." He shook his head, his face still a little pale. "Actually, Laura's research is going well. The creepers are definitely sensitive to heat. Her team is working with the tech team to modify our thermo pistols. A few well-placed thermo bullets could do serious damage to a creeper."

Okay, well that sounded good. "So, what's wrong?"

"Ah, well." He straightened. "I just got some news."

Dread coasted through Cam, settling low in her belly. She grabbed his hand. God, what had gone wrong now? "What is it?"

"It appears..." He took a deep breath. "Liberty is pregnant."

Cam stilled, processing his words. Then she broke out in a smile. "You're going to be a daddy."

The top military man in their little outpost jerked, his eyes dazed. "God. I thought that ship had sailed for me a long time ago. I never expected Liberty, never expected to fall in love, and I never expected to be a father."

He was such a strong man. One who'd fought for and protected others since the first day of the invasion. Just like her Hemi.

"You'll be a great dad," Cam said quietly.

She had a clear picture of Holmes, cradling a

child with his blue eyes and Liberty's blonde curls. Then the image morphed into Hemi holding a tiny, dark-skinned baby in the crook of one big, tattooed arm.

God. God. One day, maybe, but not yet. She wanted Hemi's child. She knew a man like Hemi valued family, and he would give everything he had to his children. Something else for them to fight for.

Cam reached out and patted Holmes on the back. "Congratulations, Adam. I'm really happy for you. I think your child is fortunate to have a father like you."

The man's blue eyes gleamed. "Thank you, Cam."

She headed into the rec room. People were settling in—pillows and blankets piled all over the place. A large screen had been set up on one wall.

She spotted Liberty's blonde head. The woman's hair always looked perfect, like a cloud of spun gold. She was talking with some other women.

Cam walked over and touched the woman's arm.

Liberty turned with a smile. "Hi, Cam."

"Your man is out in the hall, equal parts elated and terrified. I think he needs a hug."

An indulgent smile crossed the woman's bombshell face. "Nothing shakes an alpha male like knowing he made a baby."

"Congratulations." Cam knew that Liberty had changed Holmes for the better. Had smoothed out the tension the man had previously always carried, and given him something to live for.

Cam was only just truly appreciating how

important that was.

"Thanks." The woman turned and hurried out of the room.

Cam spotted her squad and the berserkers sitting with Hell Squad, not too far away from the bar.

Hemi was there, and she went straight to his side. He slung an arm around her and pulled her in close. He handed her a beer.

Nearby, Shaw held up a glass. "To Cam, who finally stopped running, and put Hemi out of his misery."

There were good-natured cheers. Hemi grinned and pressed a kiss to the side of her head. Warmth burst in Cam's chest. The love she'd been running from all her life had found her, right in the middle of an alien invasion.

Cam lifted her drink. "To nosy but well-meaning friends." She looked at her squad members who were both her friends and her family. "I love you." More cheers. "And to Hemi." Her gaze met his and she saw the love he felt for her reflected in the dark depths. An amazing gift she planned to care for with everything she had. "For being stubborn, wild, a little crazy, and for never giving up on me."

He leaned down and pressed a kiss to her lips. "And I never will, baby."

I hope you enjoyed Hemi and Cam's story!
Hell Squad continues with ASH, starring the

second of the big, wild berserkers of Squad Three. Coming in late 2017.

If you're looking for more action-packed science fiction romance, then read on for a preview of *Gladiator*, the first book in the Galactic Gladiators series.

Don't miss out! For updates about new releases, action romance info, free books, and other fun stuff, sign up for my VIP mailing list and get your *free box set* containing three action-packed romances.

Visit here to get started:
www.annahackettbooks.com

FREE BOX SET DOWNLOAD

JOIN THE ACTION-PACKED ADVENTURE!

Formats: Kindle, ePub, PDF

Preview – Gladiator

MORE SCI-FI ROMANCE

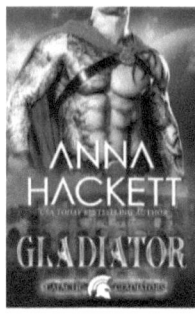

Fighting for love, honor, and freedom on the galaxy's lawless outer rim.

Just another day at the office.

Harper Adams pulled herself along the outside of the space station module. She could hear her quiet breathing inside her spacesuit, and she easily pulled her weightless body along the slick, white surface of the module. She stopped to check a security panel, ensuring all the systems were running smoothly.

Check. Same as it had been yesterday, and the day before that. But Harper never ever let herself forget that they were six hundred million kilometers away from Earth. That meant they were dependent only on themselves. She tapped some buttons on the security panel before closing the reinforced plastic cover. She liked to dot all her *I*s and cross all her *T*s. She never left anything to chance.

She grabbed the handholds and started pulling herself up over the cylindrical pod to check the panels on the other side. Glancing back behind herself, she caught a beautiful view of the planet below.

Harper stopped and made herself take it all in. The orange, white, and cream bands of Jupiter could take your breath away. Today, she could even see the famous superstorm of the Great Red Spot. She'd been on the Fortuna Research Station for almost eighteen months. That meant, despite the amazing view, she really didn't see it anymore.

She turned her head and looked down the length of the space station. At the end was the giant circular donut that housed the main living quarters and offices. The main ring rotated to provide artificial gravity for the residents. Lying off the center of the ring was the long cylinder of the research facility, and off that cylinder were several modules that housed various scientific labs and storage. At the far end of the station was the docking area for the supply ships that came from Earth every few months.

"Lieutenant Adams? Have you finished those checks?"

Harper heard the calm voice of her fellow space

marine and boss, Captain Samantha Santos, through the comm system in her helmet.

"Almost done," Harper answered.

"Take a good look at the botany module. The computer's showing some strange energy spikes, but the scientists in there said everything looks fine. Must be a system malfunction."

Which meant the geek squad engineers were going to have to come in and do some maintenance. "On it."

Harper swung her body around, and went feet-first down the other side of the module. She knew the rest of the security team—all made up of United Nations Space Marines—would be running similar checks on the other modules across the station. They had a great team to ensure the safety of the hundreds of scientists aboard the station. There was also a dedicated team of engineers that kept the guts of the station running.

She passed a large, solid window into the module, and could see various scientists floating around benches filled with all kinds of plants. They all wore matching gray jumpsuits accented with bright-blue at the collars, that indicated science team. There was a vast mix of scientists and disciplines aboard—biologists, botanists, chemists, astronomers, physicists, medical experts, and the list went on. All of them were conducting experiments, and some were searching for alien life beyond the edge of the solar system. It seemed like every other week, more probes were being sent out to hunt for radio signals or collect samples.

Since humans had perfected large solar sails as a way to safely and quickly propel spacecraft, getting around the solar system had become a lot easier. With radiation pressure exerted by sunlight onto the mirrored sails, they could travel from Earth to Fortuna Station orbiting Jupiter in just a few months. And many of the scientists aboard the station were looking beyond the solar system, planning manned expeditions farther and farther away. Harper wasn't sure they were quite ready for that.

She quickly checked the adjacent control panel. Among all the green lights, she spotted one that was blinking red, and she frowned. They definitely had a problem with the locking system on the exterior door at the end of the module. She activated the small propulsion pack on her spacesuit, and circled around the module. She slowed down as she passed the large, round exterior door at the end of the cylindrical module.

It was all locked into place and looked secure.

As she moved back to the module, she grabbed a handhold and then tapped the small tablet attached to the forearm of her suit. She keyed in a request for maintenance to come and check it.

She looked up and realized she was right near another window. Through the reinforced glass, a pretty, curvy blonde woman looked up and spotted Harper. She smiled and waved. Harper couldn't help but smile and lifted her gloved hand in greeting.

Dr. Regan Forrest was a botanist and a few

years younger than Harper. The young woman was so open and friendly, and had befriended Harper from her first day on the station. Harper had never had a lot of friends—mainly because she'd been too busy raising her younger sister and working. She'd never had time for girly nights out or gossip.

But Regan was friendly, smart, and had the heart of a steamroller under her pretty exterior. Harper always had trouble saying no to her. Maybe the woman reminded her a little of Brianna. At the thought of her sister, something twisted painfully in Harper's chest.

Regan floated over to the window and held up a small tablet. She'd typed in some words.

Cards tonight?

Harper had been teaching Regan how to play poker. The woman was terrible at it, and Harper beat her all the time. But Regan never gave up.

Harper nodded and held up two fingers to indicate a couple of hours. She was off-shift shortly, and then she had a sparring match with Regan's cousin, Rory—one of the station engineers—in the gym. Aurora "Call me Rory or I'll hit you" Fraser had been trained in mixed martial arts, and Harper found the female engineer a hell of a sparring partner. Rory was teaching Harper some martial arts moves and Harper was showing the woman some basic sword moves. Since she was little, Harper had been a keen fencer.

Regan grinned back and nodded. Then the woman's wide smile disappeared. She spun around, and through the glass Harper could see the other scientists all looking around, concerned. One scientist was spinning around, green plants floating in the air around him, along with fat droplets of water and some other green fluid. He'd clearly screwed up and let his experiment get free.

"Lieutenant Adams?" The captain's voice came through her helmet again. "Harper?"

There was a sense of urgency that made Harper's belly tighten. "Go ahead, Captain."

"We have an alarm sounding in the botany module. The computer says there is a risk of decompression."

Dammit. "I just checked the security panels. The locking mechanism on the exterior door is showing red. I did a visual inspection and it's closed up tight."

"Okay, we talked with the scientist in charge. Looks like one of her team let something loose in there. It isn't dangerous, but it must be messing with the alarm sensors. System's locked them all in there." She made an annoyed sound. "Idiots will have to stay there until engineering can get down there and free them."

Harper studied the room through the glass again. Some of the green liquid had floated over to another bench that contained various frothing cylinders on it. A second later, the cylinders shattered, their contents bubbling upward.

The scientists all moved to the back exit of the module, banging on the locked door. *Damn.* They were trapped.

Harper met Regan's gaze. Her friend's face was

pale, and wisps of her blonde hair had escaped her ponytail, floating around her face.

"Captain," Harper said. "Something's wrong. The experiments have overflowed their containment." She could see the scientists were all coughing.

"Engineering is on the way," the captain said.

Harper pushed herself off, flying over the surface of the module. She reached the control panel and saw that several other lights had turned red. They needed to get this under control and they needed to do it now.

"Harper!" The captain's panicked voice. "Decompression in progress!"

What the hell? The module jerked beneath Harper. She looked up and saw the exterior door blow off, flying away from the station.

Her heart stopped. That meant all the scientists were exposed to the vacuum of space.

Fuck. Harper pushed off again, sending herself flying toward the end of the module. She put her arms by her sides to help increase her speed. Through the window, she saw that most of the scientists had grabbed on to whatever they could hold on to. A few were pulling emergency breathers over their heads.

She reached the end of the pod and saw the damage. There was torn metal where the door had been ripped off. Inside the door, she knew there would be a temporary repair kit containing a sheet of high-tech nano fabric that could be stretched across the opening to reestablish pressure. But it needed to be put in place manually. Harper reached for the latch to release the repair kit.

Suddenly, a slim body shot out of the pod, her arms and legs kicking. Her mouth was wide open in a silent scream.

Regan. Harper didn't let herself think. She turned, pushed off and fired her propulsion system, arrowing after her friend.

"Security Team to the botany module," she yelled through her comm system. "Security Team to botany module. We have decompression. One scientist has been expelled. I'm going after her. I need someone that can help calm the others and get the module sealed again."

"Acknowledged, Lieutenant," Captain Santos answered. "I'm on my way."

Harper focused on reaching Regan. She was gaining on her. She saw that the woman had lost consciousness. She also knew that Regan had only a couple of minutes to survive out here. Harper let her training take over. She tapped the propulsion system controls, trying for more speed, as she maneuvered her way toward Regan.

As she got close, Harper reached out and wrapped her arm around the scientist. "I've got you."

Harper turned, at the same time clipping a safety line to the loops on Regan's jumpsuit. Then, she touched the controls and propelled them straight back towards the module. She kept her friend pulled tightly toward her chest. *Hold on, Regan.*

She was so still. It reminded Harper of holding Brianna's dead body in her arms. Harper's jaw tightened. She wouldn't let Regan die out here. The woman had dreamed of working in space, and worked her entire career to get here, even defying her family. Harper wasn't going to fail her.

As the module got closer, she saw that the security team had arrived. She saw the captain's long, muscled body as she and another man put up the nano fabric.

"Incoming. Keep the door open."

"Can't keep it open much longer, Adams," the captain replied. "Make it snappy."

Harper adjusted her course, and, a second later, she shot through the door with Regan in her arms. Behind her, the captain and another huge security marine, Lieutenant Blaine Strong, pulled the stretchy fabric across the opening.

"Decompression contained," the computer intoned.

Harper released a breath. On the panel beside the door, she saw the lights turning green. The nano fabric wouldn't hold forever, but it would do until they got everyone out of here, and then got a maintenance team in here to fix the door.

"Oxygen levels at required levels," the computer said again.

"Good work, Lieutenant." Captain Sam Santos floated over. She was a tall woman with a strong face and brown hair she kept pulled back in a tight ponytail. She had curves she kept ruthlessly toned, and golden skin she always said was thanks to her

Puerto Rican heritage.

"Thanks, Captain." Harper ripped her helmet off and looked down at Regan.

Her blonde hair was a wild tangle, her face was pale and marked by what everyone who worked in space called space hickeys—bruises caused by the skin's small blood vessels bursting when exposed to the vacuum of space. *Please be okay.*

"Here." Blaine appeared, holding a portable breather. The big man was an excellent marine. He was about six foot five with broad shoulders that stretched his spacesuit to the limit. She knew he was a few inches over the height limit for space operations, but he was a damn good marine, which must have gone in his favor. He had dark skin thanks to his African-American father and his handsome face made him popular with the station's single ladies, but mostly he worked and hung out with the other marines.

"Thanks." Harper slipped the clear mask over Regan's mouth.

"Nice work out there." Blaine patted her shoulder. "She's alive because of you."

Suddenly, Regan jerked, pulling in a hard breath.

"You're okay." Harper gripped Regan's shoulder. "Take it easy."

Regan looked around the module, dazed and panicky. Harper watched as Regan caught sight of the fabric stretched across the end of the module, and all the plants floating around inside.

"God," Regan said with a raspy gasp, her breath

fogging up the dome of the breather. She shook her head, her gaze moving to Harper. "Thanks, Harper."

"Any time." Harper squeezed her friend's shoulder. "It's what I'm here for."

Regan managed a wan smile. "No, it's just you. You didn't have to fly out into space to rescue me. I'm grateful."

"Come on. We need to get you to the infirmary so they can check you out. Maybe put some cream on your hickeys."

"Hickeys?" Regan touched her face and groaned. "Oh, no. I'm going to get a ribbing."

"And you didn't even get them the pleasurable way."

A faint blush touched Regan's cheeks. "That's right. If I had, at least the ribbing would have been worth it."

With a relieved laugh, Harper looked over at her captain. "I'm going to get Regan to the infirmary."

The other woman nodded. "Good. We'll meet you back at the Security Center."

With a nod, Harper pushed off, keeping one arm around Regan, and they floated into the main part of the science facility. Soon, they moved through the entrance into the central hub of the space station. As the artificial gravity hit, Harper's boots thudded onto the floor. Beside her, Regan almost collapsed.

Harper took most of the woman's weight and helped her down the corridor. They pushed into the infirmary.

A gray-haired, barrel-chested man rushed over. "Decided to take an unscheduled spacewalk, Dr. Forrest?"

Regan smiled weakly. "Yes. Without a spacesuit."

The doctor made a tsking sound and then took her from Harper. "We'll get her all patched up."

Harper nodded. "I'll come and check on you later."

Regan grabbed her hand. "We have a blackjack game scheduled. I'm planning to win back all those chocolates you won off me."

Harper snorted. "You can try." It was good to see some life back in Regan's blue eyes.

As Harper strode out into the corridor, she ran a hand through her dark hair, tension slowly melting out of her shoulders. She really needed a beer. She tilted her neck one way and then the other, hearing the bones pop.

Just another day at the office. The image of Regan drifting away from the space station burst in her head. Harper released a breath. She was okay. Regan was safe and alive. That was all that mattered.

With a shake of her head, Harper headed toward the Security Center. She needed to debrief with the captain and clock off. Then she could get out of her spacesuit and take the one-minute shower that they were all allotted.

That was the one thing she missed about Earth. Long, hot showers.

And swimming. She'd been a swimmer all her

life and there were days she missed slicing through the water.

She walked along a long corridor, meeting a few people—mainly scientists. She reached a spot where there was a long bank of windows that afforded a lovely view of Jupiter, and space beyond it.

Stingy showers and unscheduled spacewalks aside, Harper had zero regrets about coming out into space. There'd been nothing left for her on Earth, and to her surprise, she'd made friends here on Fortuna.

As she stared out into the black, mesmerized by the twinkle of stars, she caught a small flash of light in the distance. She paused, frowning. What the hell was that?

She stared hard at the spot where she'd seen the flash. Nothing there but the pretty sprinkle of stars. Harper shook her head. Fatigue was playing tricks on her. It had to have just been a weird trick of the lights reflecting off the glass.

Pushing the strange sighting away, she continued on to the Security Center.

Galactic Gladiators

Gladiator
Warrior
Hero
Protector
Champion

MORE ACTION ROMANCE?

ACTION
ADVENTURE
TREASURE HUNTS
SEXY SCI-FI ROMANCE

When astro-archeologist and museum curator Dr. Lexa Carter discovers a secret map to a lost old Earth treasure—a priceless Fabergé egg—she's excited at the prospect of a treasure hunt to the dangerous desert planet of Zerzura. What she's not so happy about is being saddled with a bodyguard—the museum's mysterious new head of security, Damon Malik.

After many dangerous years as a galactic spy, Damon Malik just wanted a quiet job where no one tried to kill him. Instead of easy work in a museum full of artifacts, he finds himself on a backwater planet babysitting the most infuriating woman he's ever met.

She thinks he's arrogant. He thinks she's a trouble-magnet. But among the desert sands and ruins, adventure led by a young, brash treasure hunter named Dathan Phoenix, takes a deadly turn. As it becomes clear that someone doesn't want them to find the treasure, Lexa and Damon will have to trust each other just to survive.

The Phoenix Adventures
Among Galactic Ruins
At Star's End
In the Devil's Nebula
On a Rogue Planet
Beneath a Trojan Moon
Beyond Galaxy's Edge
On a Cyborg Planet
Return to Dark Earth
On a Barbarian World
Lost in Barbarian Space
Through Uncharted Space

Also by Anna Hackett

Treasure Hunter Security
Undiscovered
Uncharted
Unexplored
Unfathomed

Galactic Gladiators
Gladiator
Warrior
Hero
Protector
Champion

Hell Squad
Marcus
Cruz
Gabe
Reed
Roth
Noah
Shaw
Holmes
Niko
Finn
Devlin
Theron

Standalone Titles
Savage Dragon
Hunter's Surrender
One Night with the Wolf

Anthologies
A Galactic Holiday
Moonlight (UK only)
Vampire Hunter (UK only)
Awakening the Dragon (UK Only)

For more information visit AnnaHackettBooks.com

About the Author

I'm a USA Today bestselling author and I'm passionate about *action romance*. I love stories that combine the thrill of falling in love with the excitement of action, danger and adventure. I'm a sucker for that moment when the team is walking in slow motion, shoulder-to-shoulder heading off into battle.

I write about people overcoming unbeatable odds and achieving seemingly impossible goals. I like to believe it's possible for all of us to do the same.

My books are mixture of action, adventure and sexy romance and they're recommended for anyone who enjoys fast-paced stories where the boy wins the girl at the end (or sometimes the girl wins the boy!)

For release dates, action romance info, free books, and other fun stuff, sign up for the latest news here:

Website: AnnaHackettBooks.com